As a writer, Aimee Parkison is what my younger female colleagues admiringly call a badass bitch. Daring and unforgettable.

TANK Magazine

A triumph of the imaginal in the face of a culture that would see us silenced, dead, and gone.

Lidia Yuknavitch

Previous Praise for Aimee Parkison

These are stories both about the difficulty and the intense suddenness of human connection, about the profound link that exists between being in love and being alone.

Brian Evenson

One of the most innovative fiction writers working today.

Gina Frangello

Parkison's prose flows with a subtle, musical rhythm that only prose can achieve, and then rarely ... Every sentence, every sentence, is exquisite.

Hayden's Ferry Review

Extraordinary, character-driven tales from a sublime voice that resonates.

Kirkus Reviews

These sometimes violent, sometimes visionary stories haunt the reader for days, and make the ordinary world look stranger.

Alison Lurie

Delicate, graceful, luminous, evocative.

Cris Mazza

Aimee Parkison is a shrewd, fiery, wildly poetic, politically astute writer of fiction.

Jane McCafferty

Dangerous to the bone.

Lance Olsen

Parkison treats violence, voyeurism, innocence, and guilt with imagery sharpened to its finest edge.

Publishers Weekly

Aimee Parkison, whose stories have garnered both critical praise and prestigious awards, maintains a voyeur's densely layered dynamic with the world. It is easy to get seduced as much by the sonic texture of her accomplished prose as by its startling cinematic imagery.

Review of Contemporary Fiction

Body of Evidence

Body of Evidence

Aimee Parkison

UNBOUND EDITION PRESS

Founded in Provincetown

FIRST EDITION

Printed in the United States of America

LIBRARY OF CONGRESS RECORD

Name: Parkison, Aimee, 1976 — author.
Title: Body of Evidence / Aimee Parkison.
Edition: First edition.
Published: Atlanta : Unbound Edition Press, 2026.

LCCN: 2025936082
LCCN Permalink: https://lccn.loc.gov/2025936082
ISBN: 979-8-9919575-8-8 (fine softcover)

Designed by Eleanor Safe and Joseph Floresca
Printed by Bookmobile, Minneapolis, MN
Distributed by Small Press Distribution

123456789

Unbound Edition Press
Founded in Provincetown

Contents

Exhibit 3 — The Open Secret

Exhibit 4 — The Fame Machine

Exhibit 5 — The Old World Becoming New

Exhibit 6 — Mass Attacks

Body of Evidence

WARNING

This book contains details concerning rape and sexual assault, domestic abuse, gendered violence, femicide, desecration, mutilation, torture, and acts of war.

Introduction

Body of Evidence is an artistic experiment in writing about violence. As a collection, it explores abusive relationships and complex messages about power whispered to women and girls. This book examines what can't be said, what is dangerous to say, what is necessary to say, while asking why some people remain silent and what silence means in the face of survival.

This book weaves in and out of the real, questioning the mindset and culture of a society driven by violence against women and girls. Written by a survivor of violence, the stories in this collection are often based on historical events or on lived experience of women. This writing grew from a humanities grant-funded project of nonlinear narratives investigating what remains unspoken in gendered violence, especially violence against women.

While the seeds of these stories were sometimes gleaned from actual researched events, the resulting pieces are narrative journeys that grew from these events to explore what remains unspoken in the generational echoes of trauma's aftermath. Because these are cultural narratives that define a reality of rape culture, the boundaries between fiction and nonfiction are intentionally crossed in speculative ways. Weaving hybridity of form and genre, the line between fiction and nonfiction, the line between story and conversation, and the line between narrative and confession are crossed, blurred, or erased. Antinarratives, flash fictions, flash essays, short lyrics, and micronarratives form an experimental hybrid mosaic of nonlinear prose, weaving stories both factual and speculative. Exploring the limits of realism, this mosaic of narrative scar tissue uses the speculative, the real, and the surreal as a feminist lens to view and appreciate the lives of survivors.

In writing this book, I was guided by an artistic theory that avoiding actual representations of violence would make the realities of violence against women more disturbing to the reader by showing the victims' perspective in the aftermath of attack. However, I didn't avoid certain words that are now unfashionable when discussing violence against women and girls. No matter how I attempted to veer away from the explicit, certain despicable acts had to be mentioned to examine the historical narrative subtext to rape culture.

In times of trigger warnings when "sexual assault" has become "SA" and "rape" has become "R" or just the "R-word," as a writer, I have wondered if erasing certain words is also an attempt to erase certain realities, and if so, which realities are we erasing and who benefits from that erasure where so many words are left unspoken? In writing about these troubling topics, I often wondered how far could I push boundaries of storytelling in exploring narratives that expose realities of violence against women without losing an audience of women? If empathy for characters is related to their accessibility, is writing characters who are victims of brutal, dehumanizing attacks a risk? Do the dehumanizing impacts of certain types of violence make victims and survivors inaccessible to society and to readers? If so, is this because most people do not understand, or want to acknowledge, the impact of violence in their community? Following such logic, one could argue that not writing about these situations is a risk to our collective empathy and engagement with narrative, especially since storytelling has the power to humanize the dehumanized.

If experimental fiction often lacks the transparency of traditional fiction, how do the categories of traditional versus experimental apply to characters in stories about violence — complex portraits of women or girls who have suffered the dehumanizing effects of attacks so disruptive to society, so frightening, threatening, or unacceptable to their community, that the victims become unknowable, inaccessible, silenced, ignored, or misunderstood because they exist as living embodiments of trigger warnings and words that have been erased in polite society, and therefore less transparent to those who want to understand them. How does that affect the way people tell — or don't tell — certain stories?

If authenticity comes from sensitivity, that's what makes art powerful and dangerous. A writer must feel deeply to create something meaningful and authentic. Creative risk is the same risk as with extreme intimacy. To be an artist — a creative writer — one must be open and remain open so that the pleasure and pain of others influences the work. That's what it means to create a character, a mood, a voice, or a story that sings lyrically and universally with pleasure, pain, joy, depression, sensuality, or fear — any real and deeply felt emotion that moves from the page to the reader's heart and mind.

For these reasons, whenever possible, I attempted to avoid actual representations of the violence as I imagined this avoidance might make the reality of the violence realer and more disturbing to the reader because our culture has been desensitized to graphic violence in art and entertainment, especially when it comes to the portrayal of women and girls as victims of crime in popular narratives across television, video games, and film. Ironically, as a culture we have seen so much gendered violence in entertainment that we rarely confront the reality, the political impulse behind, or the aftermath of certain horrors.

If these nonlinear confessional narratives speak toward violence without showing the actual act of violence, they lean into the subtext of unspoken trauma by downplaying the aggressors of violence and instead focus on the aftermath experienced by those connected to victims and survivors.

Where not telling a story is telling a story, where not saying is saying, *Body of Evidence* explores the subtext of what isn't said and what people say by not saying. This book of fiction is about how stories can teach us to decode silence and break through the unspoken.

In writing these stories, the following philosophy has guided me: art should create empathy by opening the audience's mind to the struggles of others. If more writers brought "poetic clarity" to the effects of violent acts on the lives of individuals, there might be less violence in the world due to the empathy for others that such narratives could create.

The "conversations" that make up *Body of Evidence* fall into the following categories: witnesses and survivors of many types of violence against women and girls, including the toll violence takes on survivors and those who love them. Some stories focus on the physical reality of the traumatized body while others leave the body behind to focus on the psychological world of the traumatized mind.

Body of Evidence explores the aftermath of romantic relationships that do violence, stranger violence, the violence of war, family violence, extreme violence, subtle violence, violence never resolved and its aftermath of transgressions, as well as how and why certain people transgress society's unspoken rules, what those rules are and the price paid for transgression when it comes to what remains unspoken — what remains unspoken between parents and children, sisters and brothers, lovers and friends as emotional scars heal and yet remain on those who have something to say.

-EVIDENCE-

FILE NO. Exhibit 1

NAME The Body

SECTIONS Body of Evidence; Coffee-Colored Buttons; Stolen Perfume; Liars; Teachers

DO NOT TOUCH

Body of Evidence

Does evidence fall from survivors like snow in winter, like leaves in autumn glinting golden in dying sun, or like dust from Grandmother's handmade curtains, dust containing the shed skin of so many people? Does evidence drift like raindrops in a storm? It's easier to talk to a stranger about why we sometimes don't scream, why hairs in an envelope, stains, laundry, and fingernail clippings tell our story more than words. If what happens to us becomes part of us, our story is written in bloodstains on a slide under a microscope, on the back of a headrest in a car, the fibers transferred onto us. Today another woman's nails have been clipped, labeled, saved, and preserved for evidence. Her clothing must be removed carefully to prevent evidence from falling. In the vents of buildings, what happened to her is pushed through the air we breathe.

Coffee-Colored Buttons

Under the bridge, the girl was wearing a tan coat with coffee-colored buttons, the kind of coat that a caring, responsible mother saved for because one coat had to last her daughter for years. A coat like that is stylish enough, but not too stylish, so it won't go out of style. Earth-toned, the coat whispered of fertile fields unmemorable, though it could fit a young girl or an old woman perfectly well. It was the sort of coat that was well chosen, showing awareness of the value of a dollar. As the train passed overhead, spotlighting the girl in moving lights through the bridge rails, I wondered how mothers, who chose items with so much care, raised daughters to live in houses where every object became a weapon, including radios, scissors, hammers, firewood, clocks, apron straps, bras, dog leashes, bleach, toasters, coffeemakers, curling irons, framed portraits, sofa cushions, curtains, mops, brooms, hot pads, dolls, train sets, coats, cookbooks and even teddy bears. My former partner, a man I loved, often told me I was lucky to be alive. I knew better than to go to the pool in a bathing suit because my bruises, black and blue, inspired friends to ask: *Why do you stay with that jerk? Didn't your mother raise you better?* She did; she really did. Mom loved me and taught me how to love unconditionally. That was the problem. When a woman who has known unconditional love starts to love someone who does something wrong, she keeps thinking he's going to change, but once the beatings start, they never really stop. After a bad night, I stood below the overpass, where headlights of passing vehicles would shine a spotlight on the girl in the tan coat with coffee-colored buttons. She was more upsetting to me than the others I had seen under the bridge, but if she had been wearing a different sort of coat, I might have been less afraid.

Stolen Perfume

Don't be afraid to mourn her by raiding dead women's closets, your mother's and sisters' closets, your grandmother's attics, your sisters' panty drawers. Go to garage sales and buy used underwear in many sizes. Pretend it's all for you. Make a girl out of cardboard tubes, old socks, nylons, used wigs, buttons, Styrofoam, paint, and cheap makeup. Dress her in used clothes, bras, lingerie, broken costume jewelry, and gloves from thrift shops. Use super glue, white glue, hot glue, rubber cement, string, clay, and wire with pipe cleaners to shape and bind her into the womanly form. Marbles can be used for lively eyes. Style her wig and apply the makeup delicately to her face to give color and appeal. Give her a name. Douse her with stolen perfume and tell her goodbye.

Liars

I turned into a chain-smoking liar because I worried if she and I talked about what really happened, it might kill her. I only wanted to take her home. It was time. She said her head was dizzy, and she didn't remember what had happened and she wanted to know. I lit another cigarette, rolled down the window, and started driving faster.

How could I tell her I had found her whispering on the snow, barely conscious at the ski resort where she and her fiancée had been vacationing when she disappeared from the lodge while looking for a magazine to read?

No one knew where she had gone or what had happened to her until I found her naked in the snow with a pillowcase wrapped around her neck. Her teeth broken. At the hospital, she sat up in bed, howling and holding her head as blood gushed from her wounds.

That was seven months ago.

The hospital just released her this afternoon after warning me and the rest of the family that she might remember nothing of what happened, and maybe that was a blessing. What they neglected to tell me was how hard it would be when she kept asking, again and again, having forgotten what we already told her.

Teachers

Carrie? Lara? Grace? Jackie? What are you up to now? It seems like yesterday that I was caring for you on the night shift. The other nurses remember. We all remember your faces turning purple with bruises and your swollen heads. Your shoulders were dislocated and at least one of you would have permanent hearing loss. At the end of a long night, I would tell you it would be okay, but I never knew what to expect. When I assumed you were dying, I just wanted you to know you weren't alone. You had been bludgeoned and raped and bound, not in that order, and your jaws were broken. You had already been brought back from death when you were found without a pulse and the responding officers began CPR. I cleaned and sutured the bite marks on your bodies. You woke with no memory of your attack because you had been sleeping in the apartment you shared. I had to explain, again and again, where you were and why you were here. At first, none of you believed me. I didn't blame you. It didn't make sense. You were all someone's teacher, someone's child.

CAUTION: DISTURBING DETAIL

-EVIDENCE-

FILE NO. Exhibit 2

NAME Precision Killings & Planned Attacks

SECTIONS A Room of His Own (Gilgo Beach Murders); Busting the Good-Girl Bubble; The Mirror Man

A Room of His Own (Gilgo Beach Murders)

Please don't go into that basement room because if you do, you'll find out why they call him the Architect. With a how-to notebook, his blueprint for murder, he considers himself a Renaissance man, a hunter, a marksman. Meticulous. Dear Rex, who organized his family reunions. A jack of all trades with an architect's precision, he planned what to do with women before and after waiting for his wife and children to leave on vacation. A patient father, a loving husband, using the basement of the family home to torture women and girls he captured. In a middle-class neighborhood, he hid in the open. In an ordinary house among ordinary houses, a regular guy doing regular things with other fathers, neighbors, homeowners, husbands, decent citizens, he is the Architect with a room of his own.

His pipeline of trauma started with his father, who beat him in the house where he lived since childhood. Never leaving, the traumatized boy transformed his childhood home into a time machine where he traveled back and forth between being an abused son to being an abusive father hiding his secret, the one thing that made his life worth living.

The Architect is both a boy and a man, a father and a son, a child and an adult. A hunter of women, he sees female bodies as toys, using them for his playtime. Years ago, he designed storage spaces with stages for captured women. Some girls were left intact and other girls mangled or broken in pieces.

But why?

Ask an angry child trying to contain his rage to avoid his father's wrath. Ask the naughty boy trying to avoid getting caught, attempting to avert his punishment with to-do lists and reminders with detailed instructions. Working as an architect, crafting an intergenerational stage of trauma, his blueprints are juxtaposed with notes on the weather and memories of the sting of his father's hands, the harsh rebukes from the father he could never please or escape. Reminders of how to avoid security cameras like avoiding his father's gaze are shuffled with memories of childhood beatings and notes on how to spot, hunt, capture, and subdue his prey — young women to be transformed into objects of play for his delight, until he has to do his homework and his chores, disposing of women's bodies.

Busting the Good-Girl Bubble

Gilgo Beach is a true horror story captured on a hard drive taken from a father's basement, a neighbor's computer, and a husband's man cave. But it's not so special or even unusual. It could happen anywhere, in this neighborhood. The Long Island Serial Killer, his basement, and his hard drive have become details of a cautionary, reverse-gender, Virginia-Woolf theory of our times: there is so much a man can do with "a room of his own." If his hidden room is on an invisible web of men and boys in a private online community, he can use the internet to share meticulous plans for women and girls.

There are hard drives everywhere containing images of women and instructions about what to do with them. Plans for the ones who are hunted and caught. One of them may be you. One of them may be me. Your mother, your daughter, your sister, your wife, your niece, your aunt, your friend, your roommate, our child, the girl who walks along the beach at night. Women who work at the store, the teacher, the waitress, a girl jogging at night.

Or so we thought, until we were comforted to discover the Gilgo Beach Killer was only targeting a certain type of woman he found advertised on a certain website — women and girls who display their bodies for men and who "dance" for money. They say it was dancing, only dancing. Nothing more, but we all thought we knew what that meant.

Since the women he killed posted ads on Craigslist, they had violated the "good girl rules." That set of guidelines used to keep women and girls safe were at the heart of why we felt immune to his violence. (If the bad girls also have rules to keep them safe, the "bad girl rules" are meaningless because they can be bargained away for money.)

We women and girls thought we were safe if we weren't doing what the "bad girls" did, if we never needed money badly enough to bargain for our safety the way Shannon did.

Bad girls were targets. Like Shannon.

We weren't like Shannon, so we didn't need to be afraid.

In our good-girl bubble, where the bad girls don't belong, we felt safe for a while, until the police, who called the Gilgo Beach killings "misdemeanor murders" because the victims were "just prostitutes," began referring to them all as "girls." It didn't matter if they were good girls or bad girls anymore. They were all just girls. Like us.

Girl 1. Girl 2. Girl 3. Girl 4.
Jane Doe, Jane Doe, Jane Die, Jane Die.

Closing the roads down on a strip of beach, the police were finding more women's bodies. People began to say the killer was a hunter, a fisherman of women.

If Jesus was the fisher of men, this serial killer was a fisher of women, just a family man, calling a victim's sister, to say, "I'm watching your sister's body rot."

A white man in his forties, blending into the community — as invisible and unidentifiable as the interchangeable numbered "girls" who were killed, routed, a true "Renaissance Man," this fisherman of women was also the architect of a blueprint for killing, a homeowner, a husband, a hunter, a father, a son, a neighbor, a stalker, a watcher of women and girls, living and dead.

How did he get so much time to do so many things when so many of the women and girls who encountered him had so little time? It's almost as if the time he stole from them went into his bank of time because this house-proud man had so much time to be many things to many people.

No woman or girl was safe because the Architect could be any man with a computer, a plan, and a room of his own. That's all anyone needed to become a fisherman of women, a hunter of girls.

The precious girl I lost once told the Architect she was only dancing. "Only dancing" for money. The same thing she told me, her sister.

Was it easy money, selling shots at a bar over the summer?

Did my sister cry? Did she beg? Why does it matter so much? What do I want him to tell me? What do I need to know, and why does he want to talk to me about her? Why? What does the Architect want to communicate when he calls?

The last man to see my sister alive could have been a man who paid to watch her dance. Even after she died, he was still watching her. The Architect was also watching me and the women in all the victims' families. When we realized this, we came together.

His calls stopped abruptly when this became about every woman, everywhere. We had to live with the suspicion that some of us could have so little time because the police, who are supposed to be protecting us, might be protecting the men who want to kill us.

We must save our own lives. From now on, Shannon is not just Shannon. Shannon is Jane, and Jane is all of us.

The Mirror Man

Some people called him the Gainesville Ripper, but we've always called him the Mirror Man.

The Mirror Man, Danny Rolling, was a serial killer who killed young female students near the campus of the University of Florida. For him, killing wasn't enough. He had to take control of dead women's bodies in rooms where they died. Posing women's corpses, using mirrors as part of his display, he terrorized an entire campus.

Even now, people still wonder why the Mirror Man decapitated women and placed their heads on shelves while keeping their eyes open, forcing them to stare at their own dead bodies. Why did he pose the corpses of women using mirrors as part of his display? Maybe Danny Rolling fancied himself an artist like Jack the Ripper or maybe he thought of himself as a magician pornographer. Did he seek to conjure sex magic in mirrors after blood sacrifice, feeling as if the mirrors had powers to replicate what they reflected many times over? In this way, every killing was not just one act of violence but many reflected and repeated to an audience.

It's all about the audience. And the eyes. All their eyes — your eyes and mine. The eyes have it. He has control of the eyes. Even now, he's forcing you to imagine it in your mind's eye, where he has inspired me to go, showing us all what we don't want to see and what seems wrong to look away from, to erase, and to forget — a message hiding the truth obscured in blood, the camouflage of gore erasing women and girls everywhere.

Being so close to the University of Florida, maybe the Mirror Man fancied himself a professor with a certain captive audience and a theory to teach his students. The women he killed became both his research and his audience. The Mirror Man believed he was creating a scene for someone else to find, teaching women and girls by forcing strangers to see something in them that they never wanted, these women becoming his legacy, no longer their own, while also forcing the women he killed to view the violence of what he had done to their bodies.

Why this passion for display? Posing was never about what he did but who he was becoming, what he taught us, and what he left behind. His legacy.

His pleasure was not so much in the violence but in the demonstration. The violence of the display, taking away consent not just from the women he killed but from anyone who came upon the scene.

The one thing the Mirror Man never wanted us to see is what I've been trying to show you — his own weakness, his vulnerability, the way his life was never enough for him, how inadequate he was, needing murder to make him feel powerful and whole, relying on bloodshed as a sleight of hand, a misdirection from the man in the mirror trying to control the narrative through the shock and awe of desecrated women.

The Mirror Man is hiding from his own reflection.

DO NOT OPEN

-EVIDENCE-

FILE NO. Exhibit 3

NAME The Open Secret

SECTIONS R&B Fairytale: R. Kelly, the Pied Piper; Weinstein's Women; F**k-Off Sister

R&B Fairytale: R. Kelly, the Pied Piper

Once upon a time when R. Kelly became the Pied Piper of R&B, girls were lured into mansions where women went unseen, ignored, and bypassed because they were no longer girls. The Pied Piper was a handsome man with a voice like an angel singing that he could fly.

We all sang his song. We thought it would save us from the plague of hopelessness.

He hypnotized girls with his music, his voice like an angel making them believe he could soar through the sky to heaven. The savior seducer transfixed girls vanishing from their families, their lives, their communities, their childhood. Out of town. Gone. Disappeared while following him. No longer seen or heard, estranged from their families, these girls were taken into hidden realms, where he controlled them with a primal fear that haunts women to this day.

We fear we could lose our children to a song. That smooth voice, silky, is the dangerous music of romance hiding horrors of men who avoid women to seek girls.

In a world where women are devalued and girls are prized, the Pied Piper is urinating into a little girl's mouth after promising to teach her how to sing his song. Even so, women love him because of his song.

He hangs out at high schools, and the girls flock to him, following him wherever he goes. He tapes himself, aiming cameras at the girls he asks to undress for women. He invites women who love him to be with little girls who pretend to be women. The women don't realize how young the girls are until after he has captured them on camera, making the women into predators of little girls.

Where men treat women like children and children like women, the Pied Piper has people helping him.

Some of his helpers have known him for such a long time, and some are women who used to be little girls who loved him long ago. They say that when he was a child, he came from another world where grown women treated little boys like men. They say when he was a child, once upon a time, there was a woman who stole his innocence. His abuser taught him how to sing about love.

His song was heard all over the world, in Hamelin, in Harlem, across oceans, on radios, in dance clubs, at high school graduations, in churches sung by the choir. Unlike the original fairytale, we paid and paid the Pied Piper of R&B until he was a very wealthy man. No matter how much we paid him, it was never enough, so he took our children.

Weinstein's Women

Think of the women who never became actresses. I was one of Weinstein's women, one of the ones who went through hell and got nothing in return. Never in a movie, I imagined myself as a movie star, and he told me I would be famous one day.

Beauty and the Beast was the guidebook used to navigate what we had to do at the hotel that became his castle. We just didn't know it. Not consciously. We didn't realize, until later, that *Beauty and the Beast* is a way to teach girls to fall in love with a man they are repulsed by with the promise that he will one day become a prince and make them a princess. It teaches women to love their abusers, to forgive them, and to seek abuse and terror in the form of a mate to reap the promised reward.

The Beast's castle lives in women's minds. It's in your mind, even now, even if you don't want it there because you've been conditioned and groomed by fairytales. As Weinstein's woman, you had to take what you learned from the fairytale as a girl and transform the ugly, hideous, stinking Beast into a prince and let him do what he wanted as you tried to control him and what was happening in your mind.

If you did it right, he would make you into a Hollywood Princess. You might even win the Oscar.

Unlike the women who went on to become great actresses, I did it all wrong.

I've always hated fairytales, and yet I fear for his daughters. Lily, Ruth, and Emma. Their father is a public figure, and they are now a part of his story, whether they want to be or not. Do they love their father, even now? Is he a prince in their minds? What will his story teach them of men and the world? Isn't it just another *Beauty and the Beast?*

Like every other father, he probably read the fairytale to each daughter a dozen times without ever realizing what he taught her.

F**k-Off Sister

When Sean "Diddy" Combs was canceled, we knew it was serious because 1000 bottles of lube and baby oil were confiscated with modified AR-15 rifles. Forget about the rifles. If those bottles had been fingerprinted along with the glassware, the names of the people those prints belonged to would shock you.

This isn't a story about him. Not Diddy. Everybody knows Diddy did it, but what about all the people at the parties who stood there as girls and boys were tied up, tied down, beaten, raped?

The ones who watched us had very familiar names and faces. We felt like we knew them. They were like family. Voices you hear on the radio singing your song, a love song, hip-hop that won't stop. Names that go with faces you see in the movies, the hero's face, the girl next door.

Names that go with faces in politics, men elected to protect you and fight for you, civil rights activists, motivational speakers, mentors, and preachers. The names of beloved actors you see playing mothers, fathers, friends, roommates on popular television shows every week, big movie stars, little movie stars, kind people, comedians, shock jocks, singers, beloved people, romantic and faithful loving couples, musicians and songwriters who wrote love songs, civil rights lawyers, policemen, wholesome names, the names of husbands and wives and fathers.

Names of pastors, good guys, beauty queens, models, and athletes from the NBA. Olympians. Oscar winners. All of them were watching as if we were a show for them, as if we were willing.

Remember when we thought famous men would save us and love us enough to make us famous like them?

We worshiped them until dreams of our own fame made us seek it like a lighthouse on a dark ocean.

Your lighthouse disappeared when Diddy rubbed baby oil on you as you waited for the ocean of darkness to overcome your eyes. Even now, you are never sure what happened because you drank the drink that disappeared time when he was grooming young boys with eyes as sad as their sisters'. As the party guests say, you were part of a Freak Off. In the recording, he and the others speak of you as if you aren't even there. You are picked up like a sack of garbage and posed like a ragdoll, unlike your sister.

Unlike your sister, who was there too long, too often, you remember that she's still looking for her lighthouse. But the light in her eyes? It's fading.

Even now, when your sister has her hands tied behind her back by a rapper, a producer, and a record executive, she's a child of hip-hop.

-EVIDENCE-

FILE NO. Exhibit 4

NAME The Fame Machine

SECTIONS The Female Exhibitionists; The Fame Machine; Antidote to the Fame Machine

DO NOT PHOTOGRAPH

The Female Exhibitionists

Once she enters The Fame Machine, the female exhibitionist who sleeps with one hundred men wants to sleep with one thousand men. Then, the next female exhibitionist who sleeps with one thousand men wants to sleep with ten thousand men. But only if it's captured on camera for clicks, fans, followers, and subscribers, for fame, for notoriety, for record-breaking profit.

Which female exhibitionist will be able to make it to one million men, and why do the fans of The Fame Machine call it "sleeping with"? Is it ever a room of one hundred and one people sleeping? No one ever sleeps like that, even as the woman's mind is leaving her body, opening herself to strangers' diseases becoming stranger with each rising body count.

In this new freak show, the circus of one woman with many men, when it comes to female exhibitionists like the woman who contracted salmonella poisoning under her eyelids, hundreds of men ejaculate on the woman's face, into her open eyes. The eyes are something to be coveted and defiled, to be owned and captured in many ways. The camera always focuses on her eyes, windows to her soul filled with strangers' cum. The female exhibitionists who do it for money and to pleasure men are "sane," but the ones who do it for free to pleasure themselves without profit are "insane" and terrifying to society. Society will stop at nothing to stop them, only if what they are revealing is not enticing.

Exhibitionism in females who do not delight and entice the male gaze is not just disruptive but threatening. Like the French woman, Blanche Monnier, who slept naked and alone in a dark attic in a beautiful mansion in the late 1800's, hidden on a litter of her own filth for decades, not seeing sunlight for over twenty years, sleeping on rotting food and feces in a dark room of blocked windows filling with rats and roaches, locked away by her mother and her brother.

But why did her family do that to her? Why did they lock Blanche in the attic for twenty-five years? That's the question everyone keeps asking, but most of the popular answers are lies. Like with most mysteries involving doomed women, people tend to make up stories of star-crossed lovers and tragic romance. Those stories are mostly lies to cover the truth that no one wants to talk about. Will anyone know the truth hidden behind the lie about Blanche loving a man from a lower class? The truth was too shameful to admit — exhibitionism without profit. Because she exposed her body at the wrong time and place, for free, she was forced to sleep with 1000 rats and 1000 roaches for 9131 days, since it was less shameful than for her to "sleep" with 1000 men in twenty hours.

The Fame Machine

The Fame Machine pulls a woman apart. She offers herself to strangers, placing her life in their hands as they open her for cameras. All those fingers and hands separate the folds of her body, turning her inside out, manipulating her flesh like peeling and separating an orange.

If the Fame Machine is a form of violence, it is achievable and profitable for women in a digital age of OnlyFans, a way to monetize female exhibitionism.

Before there was a Fame Machine, there was the opposite — the disappearing of the "madwoman" in "the attic" as she tried to manipulate her own flesh for her own pleasure, peeling and separating the intimate parts of her body like peeling and separating an orange in public. Or the asylum.

Now there's a new open-air prison advertising a Male Talent Casting Call: *1000 Men in 24 hours. To apply, email a photo of your ID and a photo of you holding your ID to your face.*

OnlyFans monetizes the female exhibitionist and is the new attic for transforming the madwoman into an entrepreneur, where she is selling a glimpse inside the open-air prison where she leaves her body, offering it to strangers as her mind wanders elsewhere, feeling none of the pleasure of the classic madwoman associated with exhibitionism, long ago, when it was still shocking and unwanted.

The Fame Machine, the attic, and the asylum — all are reactions to the same thing — the female exhibitionists — who peel themselves for their own pleasure as opposed to the ones who allow themselves to be peeled by men for the pleasure of others.

Like the attic, the Fame Machine is a form of violence, a way to deal with the female body placed on display by the woman exhibitionist. In the old days, the "madwoman" went into the attic — forced into a dark, hidden room by husband, father, mother, or brother.

Today, the "madwoman" enters the new attic online when she performs for OnlyFans, Tik Tok, Pornhub, or Twitter. She records herself or others record her for an audience of strangers who remain anonymous.

On separate screens, female exhibitionists find themselves online and, on the line, baiting each other by competing for "body counts," knowing how many men and boys — husbands, sons, and fathers, and average joes — will pay to watch and even take part, while secretly holding "body counts" against them.

In these videos, the woman's face is exposed. Her face is on display, uncovered, often revealed in close-up from all angles while the men's faces are discreetly off camera, blurred into anonymity, or even masked like phantoms possessing her, bandits or grave robbers raiding her body as she leaves it, giving it to countless strangers who become faceless to her while she's becoming robotic, distant from herself, dissociating from her body and what she won't remember.

Antidote to the Fame Machine

If there was ever an antidote to The Fame Machine and to the "madwoman" in the attic, it is Gisèle Pelicot, who was tricked by her husband into entering the Fame Machine and then invited by authorities to become the madwoman in the attic, hidden from society, as if disappearing her would do us all a favor.

Passive, unconscious, unwilling, and unaware, Gisèle was drugged and placed into The Fame Machine by her husband, who invited strange men to her house to pry her apart like peeling and separating an orange on camera. For his pleasure.

Not seeking fame or exposure, only trusting her husband in what she thought was the privacy of their own home, Gisèle didn't even know when her husband of decades carried her in his loving arms and dropped her in the Fame Machine while asking strangers to devour her.

Drugged, asleep, unaware, she was like Sleeping Beauty but with many princes giving rapes instead of kisses. Unlike willing female exhibitionists, she truly was "sleeping with" hundreds, if not thousands, of men. Because she was sleeping the entire time she was in the machine, she had no idea she would become famous.

Upon discovering the many crimes committed against her were recorded by her husband on film for display and trade, the authorities attempted to protect Gisèle from the Fame Machine. But their protection was another erasure. They wanted to remove Gisèle from the Fame Machine by sending her to the dark anonymous room in the attic, to erase her face and her name like the madwoman's face, to hide her, to protect her and us, because she might not be who we wanted to see.

Refusing to be passive again, refusing to be erased, she told her story. She said her name and allowed her face to be seen and photographed. She took control by refusing to feel shame, refusing to be silenced.

Gisèle would not go away quietly, conveniently as if she had done something wrong. Showing herself to the world, she spoke on camera to reporters while refusing to hide her face. In that moment when she faced the world to tell what her former husband had done, she was daring all women to see her for who she is, one of us.

-EVIDENCE-

FILE NO. Exhibit 5

NAME The Old World Becoming New

SECTIONS Hearts on the Ground; Louisiana, 1864; Tanks Enter the Village

ARCHIVAL: GLOVES REQUIRED

Hearts on the Ground

It's hard to know now what it meant then in the year 1500, in the letter of Columbus to the Nurse of Prince John where King Ferdinand learned that girls from nine to ten were in great demand in the New World and fetched a good price. Was that demand for girls any different in the New World than in the Old World? Did that letter set the tone for how the Old World would view the New World, was it intended to point out depravity in a new world, or to inspire certain acts committed by the soldiers and torturers once called explorers? It's hard to say what the Old World did to the New World or at what point the New World was no longer new, unless one studies history not by worlds but by women. Because soldiers seemed to be in charge even though they were following orders, it was even harder to know hundreds of years later during the American Indian Wars how it changed everything for women all over the world when Native women were gambled away by soldiers in card games and traded for knives, furs, pipes, and tobacco. Stables of women purchased by dealers were rented out to sailors. During war, soldiers lassoed women and kept them for sale or trade. Dealers of women rented out girls and sold them like horses. Women rented to sailors traveled along the waters, perhaps never able to speak for themselves in the language of their captors but knowing the real reason why soldiers were ordered to seek them out and to treat them this way. Captive women knew what soldiers never knew as the soldiers committed the worst atrocities against them. Because women were the future, there was no better way to destroy an enemy than by destroying its women. Certain women were destroyed while still alive and others were destroyed after their deaths, vulvas and breasts cut out by soldiers who stretched them over their saddles and wore them over their hats. Wearing the body parts of these women was an attempt to destroy the men who loved them. Since women and girls were nothing to the soldiers except for ways to control other men, captive girls were weaponized by those who knew the Cheyenne proverb that a tribal nation is not conquered until the hearts of its women are on the ground.

Louisiana, 1864

At the time when I was raped by a man in uniform, what happened to me wasn't seen as a crime. After all, in those days, in Louisiana, Mississippi, and Kentucky, the age of consent was ten. I was ten in Louisiana and not from one of those other states where the age of consent was as high as twelve. Whether a woman or child, in the eyes of the law, I was old enough to say yes, though I had said no. I had screamed and hollered and fought because the soldier would have no punishment besides the one that I could scratch into his feckless eyes. What did it matter if he was Union or Confederate? North or South, he was a man, and I was a ten-year-old girl. Blue or Gray, his kind were all the same to me. The North wore blue, and the South wore gray, but they were all men under the uniform. In my time, most girls didn't report men like him because we girls would be blamed and ostracized after entering a courtroom of men. Answering to the male judge and the male jury, to tell what had happened at the hands of a man, we would be interrogated by men about what a man had done. It was worse if "the woman" was only ten. Even if I had wanted to go through that trial at ten years old, just to have a chance to face my attacker in the light and to tell my story, I wouldn't be allowed. I didn't have a way to be permitted into the courtroom to speak of the crime that had been committed against me because I had to verify my age to testify. Born to a captive woman and taken from my mother at the hour of my birth, I had no way to prove how old I was in Louisiana in 1864.

Tanks Enter the Village

(present day)

After being set free by the soldiers who captured them, the women and girls live the rest of their lives knowing at any moment they could be taken again because their humiliation is like a drug that the soldiers have become addicted to using. In chains in the back of trucks, women and girls are humiliated for all to see and then erased in the days to come. When anyone attempts to tell their story, it is a lie. It is a lie, soldiers say, though captive women are offered as a reward for fighters. It is a lie, it is a lie, the women say because they don't want to shame their fathers. Girls are an incentive for new recruits, advertised with legs spread, left for dead, abducted, in chains in the back of trucks. It is a lie, it is a lie, the girls who live say, wanting to spare the feelings of loved ones mourning the dead and to have some dignity, a chance at life after being set free. They have seen boys and men, once gentle, become intoxicated by torture. These men, born with a susceptibility to addiction, have become torture addicts in war, though in peace they never would have been exposed to the drug that has changed them. Screams of women and girls excite these men like they have never been excited before. Women have seen boys become intoxicated by the suffering of girls. Girls have seen men drunk on the humiliation of women. Once certain boys and men are exposed to that high, they are forever addicts, craving the suffering of women as if it is a new street drug. Even in recovery after the war in times of peace, some soldiers will lapse, falling off the wagon, and need to attack women and girls again. By obeying orders, certain soldiers, who never would have attacked a woman or a girl in times of peace, form lifetime brotherly bonds with other soldiers in warzones where they become intoxicated by outraging women and girls on open roads, in houses, behind stores, on concert grounds, in basements, in the shadows of tanks, at gunpoint, on dirt, in the beds of trucks driving down streets on fire. Obeying orders, certain men and boys who would have been good fathers in times of peace, bring children into the world to harm women and allow their children to be raised by strangers to harm the enemy even as the children become the enemy. High on torture, the soldiers are harming a part of themselves, forever left behind. As their children become the enemy, the women and girls carry stories untold so their children will never know. Babies become weapons of war in a basement of a house, where girls and women are told that after the soldiers are finished with them, they will never want any man. Why, some captured women wonder, does the soldier focus on this business of women wanting? Even before the attack, the men fear that the captured women and girls might be capable of wanting other men in some future that will no longer exist because of what happens in the basement. Pregnant after their rape, the captured girls will each raise a soldier's child. The baby will be hers but will look at her with its father's eyes.

The child will love its mother and never understand the lie of the father. It is a lie. It is a lie, the leaders of the occupation say after a woman is taken by the commander, stripped naked and branded on the night tanks enter her village. In the basement, there are so many screams braiding into screams that no one can hear when a father offers his daughter in forced marriage to avoid her abduction, when a mother is taken from a child, when a starving girl becomes a prostitute and is no longer seen as innocent. Hunger has driven her into the arms of the men who have killed her family.

PPROVED FOR PUBLIC RELEASE

-EVIDENCE-

FILE NO. Exhibit 6

NAME Mass Attacks

SECTIONS Nassar's Girls; That Word; Down There; Men; Internally Displaced Women; Before and After; Diana, Death of a Princess in a Tunnel

Nassar's Girls

He touches us, young girls, the children and women who have been forced to delay menstruation to look like forever children. He gets us naked, which we're taught is completely normal. In the examination rooms, the walls are littered with photographs of gold medal Olympians, our heroes. Because we are hopefuls, knowing our heroes have been touched by him makes us feel what he is doing is right. Even when it feels wrong, we allow it in silence, knowing that his hands have touched our heroes.

When we whispered later that it didn't help us and didn't feel right, what he did to us in the basement, we were told, *no one else is saying what you're saying.*

Now people are saying, "Who doesn't know? Who goes to their doctor's basement?"

The ones who don't want to lose their place on the team.

The ones who sacrifice their bodies for their country, doing stuff that most girls can't or won't do, belonging to everyone but themselves.

Our bodies are our ticket.

Strong athletes who are child-size girls and women, wondering: *Is it wrong? Is it right, what he's doing?*

There's a trust between a woman and her doctor in that room where we have to push past pain, to ignore what our body is telling us.

Being a doctor gives him access to the youngest, the best.

Being cute and bouncy and smiling is a cover, not a cover up. No matter what happens, we're not to cry.

When we're racked, forced down by adults into splits as our legs are forced apart, sometimes everything hurts because being a great gymnast is like being a wounded animal. We don't show hurt. If we admit to our injuries, we lose.

That Word

I always feared that word. *Whore*, like a nightmare someone else dreamed where waking brings her back, that word has power to change her until you wonder why people started to call women that. People say whores don't have families. People say whores don't have dreams. People say whores aren't really people. After descending into the basement, you act as if you never went, as if you have no idea what the basement really is or what happened there. Even though you left the girl you once were in the basement, you spend the rest of your life pretending it didn't happen.

Down There

Don't go down to the basement. Don't let men or boys take you there. Don't even go with the boy you love, the boy you secretly want to love you. Even if he's nice to you, even if he says he loves you, don't follow him down. Down there, I'm sorry to say, there are others. Whichever boy you think you are descending with, it's never only him. If you belong to one boy, you belong to all. If you agree to go down there with the boy you like, you agree to go down there with the boys you don't. They are all waiting for you. If you walk down those stairs, the girl you are now will become the girl you were. Lost in the basement, she will leave you, disappearing.

Men

Men weren't supposed to cry when I was a child, so when they were sad, men snuck off to the vineyards at night to weep in the darkness of grapevines. I asked my mother once why the men were so sad, and she said, whatever you do, don't let them know you've seen them. Never let on that you've heard them. If you stumble upon the men in the grapevines at night, turn away, don't look them in the eyes, don't speak, don't make a sound, pretend you haven't seen them and that they haven't seen you. One day, she said, you'll know why and you'll appreciate me for telling you what not to do. Okay, I said. I understand. But I didn't understand, and no matter how I tried, I couldn't obey her. I had to go back to listen and look at the men in the grapevines in darkness. I followed the weeping in the vineyards in the night, and now I'm alone because no one wants to be near me.

Internally Displaced Women

Shouts penetrated the night. I asked Mother if she heard, and she told me it was our neighbor. “Why?” I asked. Mother said, “I don’t know how to explain, but she’s a refugee. Men she once loved made her leave her home. Don’t mention the sounds in the night. Don’t get too close or people might realize I’m like her.” I spent the rest of my life afraid I didn’t understand how men loved women while wondering how women were brave enough to love men.

Before and After

Before the fire, Mother was energetic, systematic, and quick witted. She was gregarious, a talker. After the fire, she was anxious, chaotic, and bewildered, our once immaculate lawn filling with trash fading in sunlight. Junk in overgrown gardens, no longer mown, seeded weeds through broken furniture. Half of my neighbor's face had been burnt away by a man she once loved. After the skin grafts, I watched her, not believing it was unforgivable of me. I was a child. I lived in a world where men set women on fire because men didn't like the tone of women's voices. When women said what men didn't want to hear, even if those things were true, I was always watching, even when I wasn't. I was always looking for her, thinking of her, missing her as if she were a friend, though she probably didn't even know my name. I became a piano player. To erase screams, Mother forced me to take lessons to learn to make pleasing sounds. The silence of my neighborhood became the soundtrack of my childhood. Mother and my neighbor clung to the hush between notes in my music, the thing that made my music possible by not being music.

Diana, Death of a Princess in a Tunnel

When I heard that you had died in a car accident, I didn't understand or want to believe the news. I wanted proof. Like everyone else, I wanted to approach the wreckage, to see you in shock, to open the car door and look inside, to get closer, and to reach out my hand to a beautiful woman in agony, a princess dying on her knees. Only a teenager when it happened, I wanted to see you one last time. In your final moments, there were untold millions like me, millions who thought they knew you, even though they never met you. Two-and-a-half billion people watched your funeral, but more wanted to watch you die for reasons they will probably never understand because they thought they loved you. You had difficulty breathing on your knees on the floor of the Mercedes while bleeding profusely inside your chest where no one could see without opening your body. Your heart was in the wrong place, having been moved by violence, the impact of the crash as the vehicle chased by paparazzi slammed into a beam inside the tunnel before flipping into traffic. For a moment, after becoming out of control and spinning, your world became suddenly still. Your heart had been displaced, damaged somewhere secret inside you, bleeding as strangers surrounded, staring, photographing so the rest of us could devour you with our eyes.

-EVIDENCE-

FILE NO. Exhibit 7

NAME The Scar

SECTIONS Don't Let Her Know; The Scar; Allow

HANDLE WITH CARE

Don't Let Her Know

Don't let her know you're looking. Father says, *if you brush your mother's hair, you might spy it under her curls on the back of her head near her neck. Be careful with the brush. Her curls are so very thick and the scar is hard to see. It's sensitive there. Don't hurt her by grazing it with the brush. If it hurts her, don't ask her to tell you why. If you see it, don't ask her to tell you what it is. Pretend not to see.*

The Scar

Her scar is a story that hurts worse than what made the scar. Father knows the story, and Mother knows the police know the boys who hurt her are now men. Anyone who tells the story or asks her to tell it is hurting her in a different way from the boys who gave her the scar, men pretending not to know her scar is there. Because we don't want Mother to suffer, this is a story our family never tells. The story will remain untold and die with us so that the story will no longer be a story and she will no longer be the woman with the scar.

Allow

To allow is to permit, to suffer, to tolerate, to endure, but also to submit. We were taught to be submissive and to tolerate others, not to reject or deny. If this is a confession, I concede.

CAUTION: HAUNTING MATERIAL

-EVIDENCE-

FILE NO. Exhibit 8

NAME Ghost Stories as Social Justice

SECTIONS Ghost Story as Social Justice; House, Hill; Strangers Come in Winter; Tinsel Orchard; No-Lie Cherry Pie; Making Love to Mothman; The Stinkhorn

Ghost Story as Social Justice

I don't know if Sandra Bland was alive or dead in her mugshot, but as a White woman, I'm terrified. Because of what she had to go through, I feel guilty, angry, and afraid. If my Whiteness makes me safer than Sandra Bland or women like her, I'm complicit in what the police do, even if I don't want to be, even if I feel kinship with Sandra, even if her loss haunts me like losing someone I love. I still see myself in her and admire her defiance because all my life I've been dealing with a certain type of man who becomes so angry and violent when he doesn't like the look on my face, the sound of my voice, the disrespect he claims to read in my words, in my tone of voice, in my face when I don't smile when I have no reason to be happy. Throughout my life, I've felt the room shift when suddenly my safety, my job, my reputation, and my life are in jeopardy because I've angered a man in charge — or even a man assumed to be in charge. I've been afraid to leave my home, afraid to drive, afraid to go to work, afraid to keep going. I've taken certain risks by defying men, and I never knew if it was worth it. Sometimes I planned it, and sometimes I just couldn't help myself. But I never dared to do what Sandra did. I never dared to defy a cop with a gun.

Sandra Bland haunts me because I admire her defiance and because she was a woman who became a ghost when she was still alive. There are other women like her, walking around, near us, even now. Still alive, these women are already ghosts because they have defied certain men. They are ghosts in our towns, in our cities, on our streets, in our universities, our churches, in our hospitals, in our courts, and in our neighborhoods, ghosts in the form of living women, whether we know it or not.

I've stared at the mugshots of Sandra Bland for so many hours over so many years that I can't forget her face and keep seeing it both ways. She's dead. She's alive. She's dead. She's alive. Is she? Isn't she?

Even if she was alive when that mugshot was taken, she was dead because the system had decided she was already dead when she kept smoking her cigarette when the officer told her to put it out. She was dead when she didn't smile at him submissively as he approached her vehicle. She was dead long before she failed to signal while pulling over to let his police car pass her by. She was dead when he started to follow her car in his car, long before any traffic violation had allegedly occurred. She was dead because she didn't turn off her radio fast enough when he started talking. She was dead because she argued with him when he said she was under arrest. She was dead because she was brave. She was dead because she stood up for herself and her rights, knowing what she was doing wasn't only for her but for every woman in her situation. She was dead because she dared to ask why.

A living ghost by the time she was in custody, the police found ways to make her appear alive, just long enough to try to hide the fact that they had already decided her fate. Because either way, some women are haunted by the living more than they are haunted by the dead. Haunted by the living, they become dead women walking.

House, Hill

In the hills behind the trees lives the girl I found by accident while venturing out with my butterfly net. Attempting to catch a magnificent butterfly, I captured her: dark hair dazzling like a midnight swallowtail sailing. She flickered in sunlit shadows like a wing shivering. Chasing the butterfly, we caught each other where I dreamed myself into a little girl again, my condemned house a cozy starter mansion full of golden light where cells regenerate, aging in reverse like memories. I forget why strangers say my house is haunted. If houses have stories that go untold, like lonely people, they molder in sleep, waking from endless dreams. There is no such thing as a haunted house, our fathers say. Our mothers disagree and say how dare any man whisper there are no such things as ghosts. The arrogance to claim what you can't see doesn't exist! Those who can't see us don't believe we are alive. Our fathers don't want to hear this, but certain people pretend we don't exist, that we're not real, not human, not like them. We are ghosts because they don't see us for reasons we can't understand.

Strangers Come in Winter

In winter strangers wander into me thinking I'm part of the hotel. Some strangers think I'm not a stranger. I'm much stranger than they are. Only they don't know. Not yet. They might not ever. I'm so strange they don't recognize me.

There is a child in the field. It wails like the wind. The child is a secret the night keeps from the trees and the sky. The night is a good secret keeper, but the sky has eyes and likes to gossip about the living and the dead. Don't listen to the sky. It sees too much. The sky can't be trusted because it doesn't know the difference between good and evil or the living and the dead. It has no judgment for the man who steals children.

We are all dead. Especially those still alive.

In 1979, a child is carried across the field. Don't look. It's not fair. She wouldn't want you to see her this way, naked and shivering and bleeding and mangled in the box in his arms. In the box, she can't see the sky. She sees Diana Ross.

In 1979 Diana Ross is a queen. Diana Ross is etched into the child's eyes. A girl of the disco haunts in delicious ways like a good shiver. She thrills because she is so pretty, so skinny, such a lady even as a man begins to turn her. Inside out. Diana turns the girl upside down. With elegance, her doe eyes light like stars above the field at night.

No one in the hotel knows about the child in the field in the box. If no one knows the child is there, does anyone stop to wonder what that smell is? Some guests recognize that smell.

No one thinks it's a child. Except the man who keeps coming back for days and brings gasoline and matches. The child is a girl. With my name. She is a child of 1979. Like me. Maybe she is me. Maybe that's why I'm still in 1979, that box closing on me, the lid, the sky of stars. Maybe that's why I'm stuck on Diana Ross. She was the one I thought of when the lid closed.

She saved me. I want to kiss her with open mouths when the box is burning. When the box is burning, I turn on the radio in the hotel. When the box is burning, Diana Ross sings into me like blood from the wounds on the man's face. Like blood from the child no one sees bleeding in the box, her voice fills the box in the field. No one thinks the box is anything but trash in winter.

No one talks about Diana Ross anymore. That really bothers me because in 1979 she was everywhere. Don't tell me it's not 1979 anymore. It is still 1979 and has been for decades.

1979: When the box is burning at night, strangers see its light from far away. As they drive the dark highway to the hotel, the burning box is a dot of fire flickering. The fields are so far away no one stops to find out what is burning.

Don't worry. It's never too late to save me.

When strangers in the hotel parking lot see my burning box, gorgeous flickers of incidents so terrible, they can't even begin to realize what they are seeing. They are looking right at it. They don't want to see what they are seeing, so they see something else. My face is not my face. Nor is the rope in the man's hands or the knife dull silver like fish. I still can't see his face. I never saw his hands reaching out to me, never saw his burly chin above my nose, pressing down. I never smelled the beer of his breath.

I only saw her.

In the metallic scent of blood something inside me rips me apart. Diana Ross is here with me. And inside the box, I'm not alone. She's singing, and the next thing I know we're dancing. The darkness in the box turns to light. We're holding each other. Me and my guardian angel, Diana Ross.

Don't laugh. I have something to tell you: We all make angels in our minds, but we have to find a way to allow them to rescue us. I never suffered because I knew how to call my angel, when to call her, and how to let her inside my box. I didn't wait too long. I called. She came.

Tinsel Orchard

Some of the women and girls in this shelter have long hair like my mother. Intertwined by marriage and religion, the roots and branches of family trees have become entangled with churches that favor certain hairstyles. Not every woman in the shelter is okay with that. Not every woman is submissive. The shorn woman shaved her daughter's head. Now her daughter is not mistaken for a subservient girl. She wasn't given a choice.

As we settle in for the night, I whisper to the shorn girl. I tell my mother's story in this palace of broken windows, where I am living beyond her. To make up for the life that was stolen from my mother, I work nights braiding the hair of women and girls who have run away to start new lives, to give them what my mother never had. A chance.

Mother was taken out of a secure unit of the hospital, where she ran to the roof. (It took me a long time to understand that secure units were a way to avoid saying "Psych Ward.") Our family ran out of insurance, and the doctors said my mother was stable and no longer a threat to herself. The doctor said it was time to take her home. My father grasped her arm as they walked away together. Letting go to unlock the car, he turned his back only for a moment. She ran to scale the fire escape and leapt off the hospital roof, her long hair waving like a dark flag in the wind. She lived, only to die another way. My father screamed her name, worried he was losing her. That was the one thing he couldn't stand, her running away from him.

That's not the story I will tell the girl tonight as I draw the blackout curtains the way my mother once drew her long hair in front of her eyes. No lights should be seen through the trees hiding us from the highway because no one is supposed to know we're here. My mother used to hide behind her long hair because she wasn't allowed to leave us.

Ever since I lost my mother, I've been seeing my father smelling her hair, stroking it. I'm not afraid, even though my mother has been dead for more than twenty years. He was released from prison three months ago, having served his time for second degree murder.

The first time I saw her like that, her long hair hacked off, short like a boy's, I should have guessed Mom was gone. Even after she was dead, the men in my family were still smelling and stroking her long hair. She came back to them, night after night, not as a ghost, per se, but in the form of other women. Women of long hair. That was the real reason my aunt wanted to cut my hair. I know that now, though I still haven't forgiven her, even after seeing my father, weeping, after Mother was gone. Spying on him and seeing him with a long braid, I glimpsed Mother's hair. He sniffed and clutched her braid in his bed. The braid was the one thing he begged to keep during her wake. When everyone else had left, he and I stayed behind with the open casket. He reached into the coffin with a pair of scissors to cut the braid off her head. Hiding her braid in his jacket, he left the church with me.

It has been so many years now. I fear I imagined it, not as much as I fear that I didn't. Where was my mother if not buried in the ground, and why did my father have her hair? Still too terrified to ask, I suspect my father will die soon. Whenever I'm in the house and he's gone, I search for the braid and begin to find strands of Mother's hair threaded like tinsel among the branches of the orchard. Like the trees, she links the earth with the heavens.

No-Lie Cherry Pie

"Cherry-picking season," Stella says in the evening, as she slices her homemade No-Lie Cherry Pie. Stella, with her ankle-length hair, never cut her hair in her life. Stella, whose mother disappeared like mine, whispers in the kitchen, "The little girl's mom took off last night."

"What?" I say.

"You heard me," says Stella, licking the cherry juice that drips down her arm.

"What are we going to do?"

"Make some good strong coffee to go with this pie."

Filling the pot with water, I stare out the kitchen windows facing the orchard and realize that there are parents everywhere who drop out of their kids' lives. They hide and ignore any attempts to contact them.

"She's there, again, isn't she?" asks Julia, who once sought help from the police, who couldn't do much to protect her. She had missed so much work that she couldn't make her rent and began calling crisis hotlines, whose workers directed her to where women find women and bring women to us on hidden roads through the cherry orchard.

The orchard stretches to the woods, where we sometimes see a woman hiding. She's not really a woman. Blossoming in the wind with the shadows that fear the moon, she's the thing my mother became after dying.

When I was a child, my father tried to explain how she escaped into the birds in the cherry trees, the moonlight shimmering in the inky pond on autumn nights, the wind ripping through the leaves in a whistling howl that comes from the direction of the old county hospital.

The old county hospital holds many secrets. I've often driven into its parking lot to stare into the windows of the secure ward. The hospital windows are collectors of the heartache of husbands, fathers, boyfriends, and sometimes strangers, but also a certain brightness that shines on farmers, grocers, policemen, road engineers, firefighters, bakers, carpenters, and the postman. The engineer of the train, the man in the control tower, each loves the woman he terrorizes the most.

In the locked ward, my mother is dancing. When no one else was looking, I was shorn as she crawled the white tiles to collect my hair in her hands as we stared at each other through the barred windows.

Making Love to Mothman

My great aunt, in her nineties, finally told me why she remained single her entire life. I always just assumed she was unlucky in love until I stole a glimpse of her old photograph album. She was one of those girls, the type that used to be called great beauties, or blessed.

When she told me the truth, I felt panicked because my mother confessed that for decades there had been horrible rumors about some sort of "interference" that occurred when my great aunt was a girl working on her neighbors' farm. *Interference*, it was called. No one said *rape, violation, attack.* We were told never to speak about it, never to ask her why she remained alone.

The night she died, she made a confession, still with me, haunting me, changing me.

"The mothman," she said, "often made love to me."

We were nowhere near Mt. Pleasant, so I thought she was delirious when she described him floating into her room at night, headless with no neck, glowing eyes resting on his shoulders. Taller than a man, dusty featherless wings unfurling to envelop her, he caressed her with his huge red eyes glowing.

He first found her in West Virginia, where she once visited the boy whom she loved only to be chased by his father through the fields covered in dust like pollen. The dust clung to her so that she was luminous in the moonlight: a young girl, a teenager, hysterical, ranting. No one believed her because her words didn't make sense when the field hands found her, unclothed, disheveled. Her hair and her body covered with moth scales, she coughed for days, her airways clogged with dusty pollen.

The Stinkhorn

As a child, climbing a tree in the woods, I discovered an eagles' nest and watched the eagles feeding their fledglings. High in the trees, I saw things no other person saw. No one knew I was there because I wasn't supposed to be. This allowed me to take in moments that belonged only to me and the trees.

Branches cradled me.

Climbing past the eagles' nest, I trusted evergreens. Concealed in the Douglas fir, I crouched out of sight. On my perch, I was silent. Spying, I discovered the woods.

I heard girls' laughter.

"Where is it? Where did you see it, Grace?" one girl said to another. "Find it!"

The laughter below me grew louder, nearer. Below me, six girls hovered over a small thing on the woodland floor. Pointing at it and laughing, they took off their clothes. They tossed away their shirts and shoes and socks and bras and panties. Naked and singing, they danced in a circle around a thing on the ground they called a "shameless penis."

After dancing several dizzying rounds, drunk with laughter, they dressed and skipped away.

Climbing down from the fir tree, I found the prick mushroom.

I had heard the legends, but never had seen the thing. Until then.

The stinkhorn did not disappoint. It grew in the shape of a penis with a small hole in its cap coated with greenish mucus, drawing flies and reeking of carrion.

It disgusted me, but I thought my mother might like it.

Approaching the stinkhorn for a closer look, I inhaled an odor of dung mixed with rotting meat. Gagging, I realized I was a mycophile with limits.

Around here, girls who believe in superstitions are told stories about mushrooms. Old wives' tales say dancing nude around a skunk penis will help a girl find an affectionate, handsome husband.

No matter how much I loved mushrooms, I would never dance naked because of a stupid prick mushroom. Even if I became obsessed with mushrooms, I still wouldn't dance nude before such a thing. I would never do something so idiotic.

When I told my grandmother about the skunk penis, she said, "That was the ghost of a man who died happily."

NOT FOR HUMAN CONSUMPTION

-EVIDENCE-

FILE NO. Exhibit 9

NAME Sugared Women

SECTIONS The Sugared Woman; Cellophane Dream; White Chocolate ; The Joker's Apology; The Main Street Story

The Sugared Woman

If cupcakes were flowers, I would plant them in the schoolyard garden, no Brussels sprouts or broccoli, but strawberry cupcakes, vanilla cupcakes, chocolate cupcakes, and lime cupcakes. Children would adore the garden and visit it daily to tend it with longing, attempting to single out the most beautiful cupcake growing on the vines, sprouting candied emerald tendrils, cradling cupcakes like pedestals. In sunlight, sugar dusted over icing would sparkle like gems. The smell of cupcakes baking would whisper warm butter and vanilla scenting air. Butterflies would flock from cupcake to cupcake. Each gorgeous wing would twitch, eclipsing buttercream spirals. No pests would ever go near the cupcake garden because butterflies would guard the cupcakes. Fierce butterflies would become ferocious, driving off any scavengers, ants, or flies that dared approach a single crumb. When the cupcakes were ready for harvest, butterflies would flock around the children, inviting them by dancing on air. The Cupcake Shop near the schoolyard would go out of business. The woman who owns The Cupcake Shop would lose her livelihood and her customers. Unable to sell cupcakes anymore, she would become homeless and hungry. Out of guilt, I would feed her parts of my body until I was devoured.

Cellophane Dream

During an autumn street fair in a small town with woodsy parks, fallen leaves rustle as if whispering warning. On shaded sidewalks, a little girl holds two giant ice-cream cones of perfectly packed triple scoops in chocolate and strawberry. She walks down Main Street toward her mother. A stranger with a hunting knife approaches the girl and beheads her ice-cream cones. The chocolate and strawberry scoops splatter on the sidewalk, and everyone except the girl is screaming. The girl is silent, falling into me, the sugared woman. I work in the candy factory on Main Street. Here, under cellophane, lollipops gleam like my dreams. Working in the candy factory, smelling warm vanilla sugar, girls want to eat the air, to kiss each other deeply and secretly to taste each candied breath like a treat until the manager says, *I could eat you alive.* The girls giggle as I think of the man with the knife. Terrified of rancid teeth on their flesh, they ask me if being devoured is a fate worse than death. I tell them that the madness of the flesh is only natural, a feeling some have for the young, and when the girls grow older, their flesh will no longer inspire madness.

White Chocolate

If white chocolate isn't really chocolate, we have a problem because white chocolate is my favorite chocolate in all the world. In the candy shop, in rooms of white chocolate, the woman who makes the candy tells me not to be afraid to love something too much because I just have to eat it to make it go away. I don't want to love something so much I destroy it. I need it inside me, not gone. I want the candy, to have it, but it keeps going away, inside me, like the dreams I have where a girl comes to visit and her face is white chocolate. I love her and want to be her friend. She agrees to be my friend and to sleepover. At night, when she is sleeping in the bed beside me, I pretend to be asleep. While she sleeps, dreaming, I start to eat her face. When she wakes, it takes her a while to realize her lips and nose are gone. She has her hand over the hole where her left eye used to be, the outline covered in my bite marks. I'm sorry, so sorry I forgot to eat her other eye because of what she will see in the mirror. *You ate me, didn't you?* She asks. *You ate me while I was sleeping, and you were supposed to be my friend. I never did anything to you. Why did you do this to me?* I'll never be the same because I see her the way she will be, never the same. She tasted so good my hunger must have been her fault. Now my friend is gone forever, but the hunger is back. It never goes away, no matter how much I eat.

The Joker's Apology

I'm sorry, but what I'm about to tell you is so funny that I refuse to laugh.

So, you should.

The Main Street Story

I want to forget why women in my family find the Main Street story oddly comforting, though it repulses me.

The Main Street story goes something like this:

During an autumn street festival in a small town with pretty parks, fallen leaves of scarlet and goldenrod rustle like whispers on sidewalks where a little girl holding two giant ice-cream cones, each with generous triple scoops of chocolate and strawberry, walks down Main Street toward her mother.

A stranger with a hunting knife suddenly approaches the girl before she reaches her mother, and the girl stabs the stranger with her ice cream cones, stabbing him repeatedly with chocolate and strawberry scoops in his belly, legs, and chest.

Everyone except the girl is screaming as the man with the knife falls to the ground, covered in ice cream. The girl is silent, still stabbing the man repeatedly with her ruined triple-scoop ice-cream cones. The ice cream cones are decimated, the scoops smashed on the man and fallen, melting in sticky pools congealing all over his body. The girl holds the fragments of the crumbled cones in her filthy hands, ice cream melting in drips down her wrists.

As the crowd drags the girl away, the man with the knife is laughing.

The girl's mother rushes to hold the girl and to carry her to safety before gently placing her down on the street, cradling her sticky face and hands only to see the girl, her face and hands wet with dripping ice cream, gazing up at the sky with a look of ecstasy. For the rest of her life, the girl's mother will always remember the happy calm in her daughter's eyes and wonder what her daughter saw in the sky.

I will not harm you by telling the real story.

-EVIDENCE-

FILE NO. Exhibit 10

NAME Dancing

SECTIONS – 1983 – ; Dancing Girls

HOLD: TEMPO

— 1983 —

Michael Jackson is dancing "Thriller" with Webster, and there's nothing disturbing about a man wearing one glove causing so many women to fling their panties. The gloved one is singing about pretty young things while dancing with young boys. Michael is looking prettier than any girl who thinks the song is just for her, but girls don't feel they need to compete with his beauty. His sparkling glove gives them a funny feeling inside because he's a man and in 1983 men aren't supposed to be pretty, not prettier than women or girls. It's not okay for a male to think of another male as a PYT in 1983. When Michael dances with Webster, the world loves it, and no one thinks it's wrong because in the song the PYT is always a girl and Michael is dancing with her. Michael's weirdness makes men, women, girls, and boys love him because everyone thinks Michael is harmless and gentle and childlike but capable of lusting after PYTs, who are young girls. It's okay for men to lust after young girls in 1983, if they know what's what, and songs on the radio teach us what PYTs are for. No one admits that Michael is a PYT — the most successful PYT of them all. Because it's 1983, everyone is fine with young girls being called PYTs, but no one is okay with a boy or a man being a PTY in public because boys can't be PYTs, or at least most people (especially boys) haven't thought of boys that way. 1983: to call a man or a boy a PYT is to risk murder. PYT is not a violent song until one hears it decades after Michael Jackson dies. The song becomes a different song over time. Though the lyrics don't change, the meaning does because we listeners are changing. PYT is full of messages everyone hears, and few understand until we understand all too well. Few people hear the song the way they used to, even those who want to. It's pop rock, like candy, poisoned. R&B but a little bit rock 'n' roll, it still rocks but doesn't roll the way it used to. It rolls another way. Listen to it long enough, and you'll hear the rhythm fighting the blues because a song isn't a song when a person is a thing.

Dancing Girls

The yellow house, perched atop a slight hill far away from the neighborhoods, was clearly abandoned and had been vacant for years, so layers upon layers of dust concealed me. The windows had been broken so completely many had no glass. Bent nails holding warped boards stretched precariously across the frames near slender curving brown mushrooms blooming in dainty tribes.

"Anybody home?"

I didn't answer.

A mauve gramophone rested on a skeletal table with three hooked legs. Scribbled notes — crumpled, torn, browned by rain — scattered like leaves in the far bedroom where the queen-sized iron frame rusted against crumbling walls. A mattress, half burnt, was propped beside a slouching red door. A black-and-white photograph of a huge man bleached by sun, the moth-eaten lace of a wedding veil sewn into a translucent child's dress, and a harmonica full of dirt were hidden inside the mattress.

Melissa, who had stumbled like a baby barely walking after she was struck on the head, didn't want to be there. I was too worried not to follow.

The lady in black opened the iron door, hinges screeching like birds.

Melissa reached out to me. The lady in black held her under her long dress. The dress swept the floors as we swayed.

Melissa kept her eye down to watch the light on her feet.

I clung to the thick cloth, my face hot, my breath wet against Melissa's mouth.

TRAINING MATERIALS

-EVIDENCE-

FILE NO. Exhibit 11

NAME Good Women

SECTIONS STAR House; The Good Woman; The Not-You; Sister Replay; Bastards and Beauty Queens

STAR House

(for Marsha P. Johnson)

If the killing of Trans women doesn't erase them or force them into hiding, will the murders ever end? Will anyone create a safe place for them like STAR House? I wonder, will there ever be another STAR House like the one Marsha built?

Maybe the three-hundred-fifty Trans women killed last year are why Marsha P. Johnson created STAR House decades before today's young Trans people were born.

Marsha, who always had a smile for everyone, even strangers. Marsha, who didn't have a home. Marsha, who went out into the night. A woman like her, where does she sleep?

Unhoused in Manhattan's Flower District, she once slept under tables of Stargazer lilies, lilacs, and hothouse roses. Sleeping under a table where birds of paradise were sorted, she dreamed explosions of yellow forsythia and awoke to weave fallen blossoms into corsages and crowns.

A volatile saint banned from certain bars, she started her journey as little girl who began wearing dresses at age five and married Jesus when she was sixteen. Jesus' bride, still in high school, she grew up as a childhood survivor of rape. Knowing the harassment of boys and the dangers of transphobia, Jesus was the only man she could ever trust. That's why she married him, running away with him to the city, a bright light on the streets at night. The streetlight, her spotlight.

Streaming stray petals, she walked in the fragrance of eucalyptus shoots. Under the shadows of skyscrapers, her

Street Transvestite Action Revolutionaries sheltered young Transgender people rejected by their families. They became her family as she built a series of STAR houses for them in deserted motel rooms, derelict structures, neglected big rigs, and vacant vans.

In the back of borrowed trucks and in dilapidated dwellings in unoccupied buildings, she and her tribe slept in safety while awaiting eviction. Each time their house was destroyed, they still had each other and Marsha, who kept them together, creating more houses, even after being arrested over one hundred times.

Lighting candles in churches, praying to Jesus, wearing velvet and throwing glitter, raped, arrested, and evicted too many times, Marsha tossed off her gowns and walked naked up Christopher Street. Arrested, hidden away, and confined with chlorpromazine, she was stolen from herself, only for a little while.

STAR house existed no matter how many times people tore it down. Even if only in her eyes, it was there.

Hustling in New York while wearing long elegant thrift-store gowns the color of roses, the Mother of STAR House could be recognized by her crown of flowers. Armed with chrysanthemums, poppies, and trumpet flowers, she ventured out into the night to feed the children of STAR House.

Welcome, welcome, come home to STAR House, she said to her family. In STAR House, Marsha's welcome cut through shadow plays of grief and pain. Circles of candles and flowers cut through vicious memories of those who had hurt her and were still waiting to hurt her.

Did she ever escape? Where is STAR House now? Is it still in her eyes? Can we ever find it?

I want to ask her: What happened to you, Marsha? Did you ever escape your torment as you helped others to escape? Is there any way of knowing? Even after you died and your body was found in the river, the stars sparkling on the water were a reminder of the brightness of the galaxy of Trans children in constellations, waiting like wishes on the falling stars burning like the ghosts of your love for the adopted family you welcomed into STAR House.

The city smolders even now, though when you arrived at Stonewall, it was already on fire. In the legend of the uprising, was it a brick you threw or a shot glass at a mirror? Pay it no mind because in a house of stars, the ceiling is the sky, and no one can ever take the stars in the sky away from you. Not even the sky reflected in the Hudson River, where the stars wink and call in silent flickers in the night, *Marsha, Marsha. Come home.*

The Good Woman

One night when I was a young woman living alone in my first apartment, I heard her screaming. Her screams filled me with dread. I assumed the sounds were only a wounded animal.

The next day, I asked my neighbor if she had heard the sounds in the night.

My neighbor told me it was a woman being attacked three streets away but the woman's screams carried far and clear so that they sounded closer to us.

By who, I said.

Who knows? My neighbor said.

But why did they do it?

Because she is a bad woman.

Why is she bad? What does that mean?

Oh, I don't know how to explain it, but everyone who knows her knows she's bad. One day, you'll see her and understand. If you do see her, try not to get too close or act too friendly.

Why?

Because people might think you're like her.

The Not-You

As a teenager, I explored old junkyards and found a graveyard of cars on my way to the river where we lost ourselves in each other until there seemed to be no boundaries between us. Loving in the sparkling waters, I won't say what happened there because I've spent the rest of my life not saying. The river flowed to the edge of town where the woods began. In that place between the town and the woods, where the woods became fields, the river threaded fields all the way to the city. Men chased girls as hunters tracked deer, wild turkey, and feral hogs. My grandmother told me she was hunted where fields became night. The river to sundown men, flesh dressed in blood, hardened like old bread by dawn when they found what they never wanted to see — girls who had learned things their fathers didn't want them to know. "Grandmother," I wanted to ask, "did you become not-you, the way I became not-me?" I never had the nerve to ask because I didn't want to risk becoming a stranger. Once I stopped being me, washing blood off in sparkling water, I befriended a pregnant girl. I ran away to Grandma because the girl sent me to her. "Once a girl has a baby," Grandma said, "men pretend not to see their eyes in the baby's eyes." (I see you.) Grandma lost the girl she had been when she held the girl she called *daughter*. My mother. Grandma tells stories of those days when she was hunted along the river, and I see the girl my mother once was staring through her eyes, speaking to me in wordless ways. *Run. What are you doing? What are you waiting for? Run! While you still can, run, girl! Run!* I want to tell her why I ran to the river.

Sister Replay

I made the mistake of telling. It kept replaying in my brother's mind because he wasn't there. I suspected no one would ever catch him. I wanted to be that way. On the news online, his stolen motorcycle crashed at 80 miles per hour during a police chase. My brother disappeared, a meat crayon. His body, with the motorcycle, vanished in smoke from the burning van. The camera panned to shop windows, empty sidewalks. Cops exited their vehicles before walking through smoke. I paused the video to search the asphalt. In midair, my brother somersaulted like an acrobat in rust-colored spray. His jeans tore free as blood clouds streamed. Liquified organs escaped his body painting a burgundy stain on sidewalks.

Bastards and Beauty Queens

Once, you were a beauty queen, the most beautiful girl in town. Men fell at your feet. They begged to dance with you. You could dance across any floor. Now, you're an old woman, living alone and trying not to look at the dirt and cat hair feathering your cracked tile. Take comfort in knowing your feet have been around, babe.

Your legs were once so slender men called them pins – it doesn't matter what they called them, just that they never called them legs. Because they were something better and different from mere legs. Now, it doesn't matter that no one stares at your fat legs anymore and that if people talk about your legs, they're just chunky. Your legs have been around, babe.

When people mention your name to the men who used to love you, they all say, who do you mean? What's her name? Say that name again? No, that doesn't sound familiar. I don't know her. I knew no one by that name. Take comfort in knowing they all know your name. They only lie about it because your name has been around, babe.

In that old movie scene, you were breaking all the girls' hearts (secretly) after breaking all the boys' hearts. Strangers kept rewinding your scenes and saying, she's the one. Now, they look at you and think she's no one. Your movies have been around, babe.

Though they were once longing for you, waiting for you to invite them in, they all said it happened too suddenly when you waved them into your bedroom. There were a lot of boys and men but never anyone special because they whispered your ashtrays had been around, babe.

Tonight, you're waiting on the dance floor alone, about to go home, when a young man walks to you and asks you to dance. As your son dances with you, all the women stare. Watching him, the men are whispering, he's the one, he's my son, the kid moves like his mother but has eyes like mine.

BEHAVE WHILE READING

-EVIDENCE-

FILE NO. Exhibit 12

NAME Daddy Issues

SECTIONS Genie, the Forbidden Experiment; Passive-Aggressive Daddies; Hollywood Sons and Daughters; Jamie Duncan

Genie, the Forbidden Experiment

Feral child, your father disliked children. Finding them noisy, he punished you for making sounds so that you never learned to speak. He thought you shouldn't be alive, that you were slow and unintelligent, and that you wouldn't live to see thirteen. As if he made a bet with himself, he wanted to stack the odds in his favor, tying you naked to a chair in your room in the dark, leaving you there on a plastic toilet. A child's toilet in a makeshift harness he forced your blind mother to sew. Never speaking in words, wanting you to be afraid to speak or make sounds, he needed you to fear him and to understand him as a guard dog, not human.

Because of what he did, much of what is not known, you would always be afraid of dogs, though you had never seen a dog before you were released. And you would always love men, even as a child, in the way certain women love men. He swore he never sexually abused you, but no one could explain why as a child you developed the habit of approaching strange men and fondling yourself in inappropriate ways, inviting them to touch you.

Because you couldn't speak or read or write, because he assumed you wouldn't live and that you were mentally defective, he gave himself permission to do as he wanted. Assuming you were the safest victim, he made sure that you would never be a credible witness to your own story.

Because you had never seen a dog before, no one could explain why you were so afraid of dogs, until they discovered your father purposely grew his fingernails long to scratch you if you made a noise. He would lash out in silence, clawing with his fingernails on your naked body. A sudden slashing, scraping so fast you might not see it until you felt its sting and tasted blood. He wanted you to fear him. He needed you to fear him. If he had to communicate with you, he made sure not to use words. If you dared to make a sound, he stood outside your door, growling.

You thought your father was a dog.

Soon, you learned not to make a sound. You learned not to move your mouth, even to chew food. You would swallow only liquids. If given solids, you refused to chew but just silently held the food in your mouth for hours to dissolve.

Hours dissolved in that room where there were no toys, no games, no television, no light, no other children, and no people. Not even your mother was allowed to enter the room or untie you. Your legs didn't develop because you spent so many days and hours sitting, tied to that chair. The chair became a part of you. Eventually, even when untied and allowed to stand, your body was trapped in the sitting position, as if the chair was always beneath you. Finally allowed in the light, you wanted to go back in the dark. Naked in the dark, you waited for nothing and no one.

Passive-Aggressive Daddies

When I tell you I'm having your baby, you ask me if I want you to say you're happy, and I wonder if our daughter will be as passive aggressive as her daddy.

Is being passive aggressive a genetic trait, is it learned, or is it just a gift some have?

When the doctor confirms my suspicions that we're having a baby girl, I want her to have everything she wants, even if I don't know what her daddy wants.

Now you're working every day to give me money, so I'm no longer the perfect girl for you. The perfect girl is inside me, growing every day, waiting to meet us and you tell me you don't want to meet her because she wasn't invited into your life.

She should have waited for her invitation. She's impolite, unwanted, an intrusion. You didn't ask for her. You don't want her. She's coming anyway, like some uninvited guest who will never leave for eighteen years.

Please quit thanking me for ruining our lives. Quit asking if I'm happy. I didn't mean for this to happen. It did. Stop asking me to tell you why.

Why are you so passive aggressive, daddy? Why do you do the things you do? Why do you work so hard to give me money when you're hardly even working? It's not for me. What I want doesn't matter anymore than what you want. All that matters is everything she wants.

Hollywood Sons and Daughters

I prayed for a daughter with hair the color of Marlene-Dietrich gold and Liz Taylor's violet eyes, but I got a son with Greta Garbo sighs coming from James Dean's ashtray mouth. I dreamed of a girl with Betty Grable legs and a Marilyn Monroe cheesecake figure, but I got a boy with Meryl Streep class and Jack Nicholson sleaze. I wished on a star for a girl with Ingrid Bergman's voice and Cary Grant cool, but I got a boy with Brando's menacing stare and Audrey Hepburn's style. I longed for a girl with Katharine Hepburn's dry wit and Sidney Poitier's diplomacy, but I got a boy with Orson Welles' temperament and Grace Kelly's sex appeal. I dreamed of having a girl with Charlie Chaplin's sense of humor and Olivia de Havilland's longevity, but I gave birth to a boy who drank like Vivien Leigh and possessed the empathetic intelligence to tell me I had the mothering instincts of Joan Crawford. I asked for a girl with the professional judgment of Anthony Hopkins and the vivaciousness of Sophia Loren, but I cradled a boy as sensitive as Judy Garland and as subtle as Mae West. My boy is as pretty as Rita Hayworth and as sultry as Lauren Bacall, but I wanted a girl who danced like Shirley Temple and cursed like Clark Gable. That's why I laugh like George C. Scott, smoke like Bogart, eat like Gary Cooper, and dance like Gene Kelly when my son turns his music on and tells me I have Bette Davis eyes.

Jamie Duncan

Jamie Duncan loved to hitch more than any girl at Northwest High School. Jamie loved truckers because her father was a trucker. She idolized him. She wanted to marry a trucker, to be with truckers, to go on the road.

When her father found out she was hitching rides from truckers, he threatened her.

We were seniors when she disappeared, just went out on the highway and never came back. Her father killed himself three years later, stuck a shotgun in his mouth, and used his big toe to pull the trigger.

I used to look for Jamie everywhere I went, especially when traveling. For decades, I kept thinking I would run into her on the highway, that we would cross paths at a truck stop or gas station or rest stop.

I thought I saw her on a roof of a motel along the highway, smoking a cigarette, in the low sun. It was another girl.

After I became a grandmother, I was dropping off old clothes at a church and saw a woman working in the charity closet, and I said, "Jamie? Is that you?"

She said she didn't know anyone named Jamie, but I kept coming back to that church, and she kept watching me.

"Where have you been?" I finally asked.

She followed me into the kitchen of the church, where the preacher's wife made coffee with reused coffee grounds that tasted of rust.

"Why didn't you come back home or at least get in touch with anyone? We were looking for you, people are still looking," I said.

She glared at the school ring I wore on a chain. She used to wear one just like it when we went to high school together.

"I need a cigarette," she said.

I followed her out the back door, down an alley behind the church, up a metal ladder to a fire escape to the roof of a bank, where she lit up a cigarette to smoke in the low sun. She smoked, gazing at the highway in the distance, feather clouds on a bright blue sky, wispy white trails. She blew smoke, saying nothing, never glancing my way.

"Look at me," I said.

She dropped her cigarette and charged at me, pushing and shoving. I almost went over the edge.

-EVIDENCE-

FILE NO. Exhibit 13

NAME My Mother Called It Terror

SECTIONS Sleeping Babies Lie; My Mother Called It Terror; The Smokehouse

IDENTIFICATION REQUIRED

Sleeping Babies Lie

One of my clients is a medical technician, who carried the infant out of the daycare where I work. The medical technician, after dropping off his own toddlers, accompanied the infant's father with the infant's mother. She stuck her hands in her denim pockets before he was charged. He had been trying to sleep, and the baby was crying. They decided to take the baby to the daycare and keep it wrapped in its blanket, asking us not to wake the baby as they pretended it was sleeping. This way, eventually, when we daycare workers realized the baby was dead, the parents could say it was alive when they left it with us. Thank God we had the medical technician dropping off his own kids. It was too late to do anything for the infant, he said, but the parents had to know that their baby was gone before they brought it to us. It had been too late for so long for them. Both parents were living in a one-room apartment with four children all under the age of five. Here are the details that no one but me will tell you about the situation: 1.) both of the parents were so beautiful it hurt to look at them 2.) both of the parents loved each other and were teenagers when they first became parents 3.) both of the parents loved their children 4.) even parents who love a child are capable of killing that child 5.) the wife was pregnant again 6.) people can be dangerous when they need to sleep 7.) sleep deprivation is torture 8.) an innocent child can torture her father, who is torturing her mother with his love.

My Mother Called It Terror

All my life I've wanted a condo close to everything in the city so I can just walk, having a little view of the buildings, but I don't like to see into my neighbors' windows or for my neighbors to see into mine. I never thought so much about privacy until after I moved in, but I will never tell my mother, who keeps asking, "Who would want to live in a condo?" I tell her that a lot of people do, but not many people I know can afford one. "Why would you want that?" My mother asks every time I tell her I have moved in, but I never mention the feeling that someone is watching. My condo windows have no curtains because part of the value is the view. It's hard to explain things to my mother. It's easier sometimes just to throw it right back, just to respond to her question with another question, like, "Why would anyone want a house? Why would a man want to breathe air?" I did ask her that once, and she gave me a strange look, far away. "Mom?" She sucked in her cheeks. "I was just thinking of Uncle Terrance," she said, "because it was hard for him to breathe in that bag." "What bag?" I asked. This was the first time I ever heard of any Uncle Terrance. "Terrance, your uncle," she said, "was arrested for terrifying women in their apartments. His lawyer convinced the police to cover his head with a brown paper grocery bag after his arrest when officers led him down the street so photographers could take his picture for the newspapers. His lawyer cut square holes for Terrance's eyes so no one could see his face, not even the photographers from the newspapers." Well, great, I thought, assuming I was related to a pervert. "The creep," I said. "He was innocent," Mom said, "and the bag helped with fairness and accuracy of identification in the police lineups." The pervert who began attacking women was never found but was later indicted based on DNA. If the creep is ever arrested, he can be charged with sexual assault. But my mother never called it that and wouldn't say those words. My mother called it terror.

The Smokehouse

Why are there so many murders, and why doesn't Dad want to talk about it? I want to ask, but I suspect the inconvenience of having to talk about murders is what makes some murders possible.

Great Grandma doesn't mind talking about death.

Dad can't stand talking about it.

Mom's Mom, Great Grandma's eldest daughter, was run over by a bus. She was shoved into traffic by a stranger while riding her bike to The Smokehouse, a community theater where she was an understudy in a play about a woman who would change the world.

-EVIDENCE-

FILE NO. Exhibit 14

NAME Women Who Tried to Change the World

SECTIONS Grab 'Em; Failure to Signal

LISTEN CLOSELY, LITTLE LADIES

Grab 'Em

Some men prefer the finger to the penis for reasons known only to them. Perhaps that's why millions of dollars have been spent in government grants with teams of scientists studying fingers in relation to the penis.

In some courts, it's a matter of law. When it comes to rape, does the finger even count? Does it count the same as the penis? Should it? Why, or why not?

Like penis size, hands do matter. This is according to scientists.

Retruth: *It has been reported that the length of a man's index finger is a fairly accurate indicator of his organ size. But one recent study has suggested that men with shorter index fingers in relation to their ring fingers were more likely to have a larger penis. Researchers measured the index fingers and penises of 144 volunteers and found that the bigger the difference between a man's index and ring finger, the bigger his penis was likely to be. This may have something to do with prenatal hormone exposure.*

This may be the reason why. But that can't be right because a rapist isn't kind to women and another study says that men with short index fingers and long ring fingers tended to be kinder to women. (**Another retruth:** From the same *Psychology Today* article, "Like Penis Size, Hands Do Matter: It's the index finger to ring finger ratio, stupid" by Dr. Mark Borigni, a board-certified rheumatologist who has devoted his career to treating illnesses that cause chronic pain.)

Scratch that theory.

Here's another theory: Maybe it is all a matter of time, efficiency being the key to the success of the serial finger rapist. Fingering is faster and doesn't expose the aggressor.

If timing is everything, if it's a numbers game, maybe the finger rapist is aiming for a higher body count while hiding his own flaws by not exposing his body.

Maybe he just couldn't get hard. Or stay hard.

How long does it take? Less than three minutes.

180 seconds to change a life.

2.5 minutes. 150 seconds to make a woman different.

Minutes, seconds. Inches, centimeters.

The echoes are never over: shame, mixed messages, confusion, doubt, guilt.

The attack on a woman's character takes years, decades. Defamation can last a lifetime, even longer, if she dares to speak out ... about the finger.

Silenced, humiliated, and slut-shamed, a woman who accuses a man of rape is a problem for society. The problem with his finger is that everyone believes her, especially those who pretend not to believe.

His best defense? *I don't know that woman. She's not even my type.*

My finger doesn't want her. My finger doesn't know her. My finger doesn't want to know her. My finger doesn't fancy her. She doesn't make it twitch. My finger doesn't remember her or recognize her face.

Why would the President of the United States have such troubling fingers? Why are his fingers so unkind to women? Why "grab 'em" unless violation is its own reward, the look of terror, shock, revulsion, disgust an aphrodisiac so much more appealing than seduction or the consent of the willing. Violation by finger is the only thing that makes him feel powerful, teaching the victim that she is no one and nothing so that even a finger can change her life forever. If she is no one, she is caught in a conundrum of a victimless crime since there is nothing he isn't allowed to do with his hands and no one to stop him from assaulting a nobody like her.

After all, it's just a finger! Although she will remember his face, he won't remember hers. She looks like his wife, his daughter, his ex-wife. And in his mind, to him, she is all of them. When asked to identify them in photographs from decades ago at the time of the assault, he identifies her as his wife and his wife as a stranger. They are interchangeable until she stands up to him by saying her name: *E. Jean Carroll.*

Failure to Signal

In the United States in some towns where the penalty for failure to signal is death, we're still haunted by Sandra Bland's mugshot. Some of us have spent hours looking at photographs of her face, trying to determine if she was dead or alive when the mugshot was taken, if the image has been doctored, and if so, which version of the mugshot has been altered, by whom, and why.

While some women are haunted by the living, some are haunted by the dead. Trying to get on with our lives while pretending everything is fine, we're as terrified as children because none of it makes sense, not knowing whom to trust, if we are the criminal or the victim, the innocent or the guilty, not knowing what the penalty is for driving while a woman, while Black, for smoking a cigarette in a car, for being uncooperative, for becoming irritated at being treated with disrespect, for refusing to exit our own vehicle when we've done nothing wrong. Right or wrong doesn't matter with certain men in certain situations where the most wrong a woman can do is to be right.

Officer: *Are you done?*
Sandra: *You asked me what was wrong, and I told you.*
Officer: *Ok.*
Sandra: *So now I'm done, yeah.*
Officer: *OK.*

As a White woman, my terror is nothing compared to the terror of Black women, who have suffered more and differently than I will ever suffer or imagine.

Officer:	*You mind putting out your cigarette, please, if you don't mind.*
Sandra:	*Now I'm in my car, why do I have to put out my cigarette?*
Officer:	*Well, you can step on out now.*
Sandra:	*I don't have to step out of my car.*
Officer:	*Step out of the car.*

Race is never in the rearview mirror, but neither is gender when a woman is disobeying a male authority figure. I know. I've seen certain men get so angry at me over little things, perceived slights. Some of them don't even know me. It started when I was a young girl. Strange men approached out of nowhere at night if I was walking home alone from the library. Confronting me, lecturing me, these men were asking me what was wrong because I didn't smile at them. Men who ask women and girls, *why aren't you smiling*, or, *where's my smile*, are self-appointed police officers of women and girls. Some men assume that women and girls must behave a certain way. They assume that a woman or a girl should smile at men and need a warning if they don't. Any girl who doesn't smile, if she still refuses to smile after their warning, will see how angry these men become. And these men aren't even cops. They don't have badges or the authority of the state to police girls' smiles and women's attitudes, but they see it as their God-given right.

So, at night, even when I don't want to, I smile at the strange men who tell me to smile. Even if I hate them, if they smile, I smile back. Even if they terrify or disgust me. Even if I have nothing to smile about, I smile on command. It's an old habit I despise. Even if my heart is breaking, I smile for the men who expect me to smile and for men who tell me to smile because I grew up in a house where it wasn't safe not to smile at men.

I smile because I want to live. I want to walk away, unharmed, but I drop my smile as soon as my face is out of view.

Because I grew up in a world where girls were ordered to smile on command, I want to speak to Sandra Bland to thank her for what she did but also to go back in time and to beg her not to do it because she was braver than most women and that's why she died. With cops, it's even worse when a woman defies him because in our society men are supposed to be in charge and if a man is disrespected by a woman, he must defend himself because a woman who doesn't smile at him, a woman who doesn't speak sweetly and softly, a woman who dares to be distracted from his words by enjoying a cigarette she lit and paid for with her own money is not a woman who is interested in him or even afraid of his gun. She's a woman with the power to take everything away from him by damaging the one thing that matters most, his pride. She's what his taser is for, so he can "light her up" like that cigarette she refuses to extinguish.

MAY PROVOKE SCENT MEMORIES

-EVIDENCE-

FILE NO. Exhibit 15

NAME Phantosmia

SECTIONS Phantosmia; Breathe; Consensual; The Tangled Woman; Terror, the Perfume; Terror (Ad); Voice Over Documentary; Fragrance Pyramid

Phantosmia

Sometimes it's a scent you smell without knowing, a pheromone that changes the atmosphere more than any perfume, no matter how cheap or expensive the bottle. If a woman could bottle a scent like fear, she might capture it in a bottle of dark purple glass, a vintage perfume bottle with an old-fashioned elegant mister. Her mister might spend hours investigating her underarm secretions along with the secretions of other frightened women and girls, who have been terrified by men, boys, and each other.

In glass bottles with flexible stoppers, a terrified girl could pump air from her vagina into a liquid to create a mist of her terror with atomizers of silence. A scent like Fear, the perfume of terror, captures the essence of walking alone at night, the essential oil extracted from a woman's armpits, her cunt, beneath her breasts.

The fear of women and girls could be captured through steam distillation, douching, solvent extraction, enfleurage, maceration, the expression misted through a carrier oil like sweet almond, coconut, or jojoba, combined with 100-proof alcohol, a spoonful of piss, several dozen drops essential cunt oil, eight drops arm-pit top notes, two drops middle notes trickling between breast cleavage, and finally the fix drops in base notes of feminine toe sweat combined with misted screams. All these ingredients, tunneling through a small funnel and coffee filters, would drip to dark-glass bottles of captured fear.

Terror, the perfume, taken from the inner labia and underarm secretions of petrified women and traumatized girls, might offer many complex notes of a female floral, citrus, ocean, metallic, blood, salt, garlic, sour, bitter, acid, delectably repugnant vinegar, a chemical signature of pheromones unconsciously detected during female fight-or-flight, often referred to as "Phantosmia."

Breathe

As a girl, I first sniffed it on my skin and on other girls whenever strange men followed, cornering us, leering where we had nowhere to hide.

Even now, guided by the sense of smell, I lose myself in the funk of cat breath as cigarette smoke lures me from my intentions. A thumb piercing an orange skin in citrus mist awakens me like the roach and the struck match stolen from a ramshackle diner because I want to remember how much I loved drinking coffee with you from a cup of Buffalo China.

If I could remember not to be forgotten, I could remember why I didn't want anyone to smell the real me. I hid from you because I loved you, even though you terrified me. I didn't think you could ever love the real me.

Since I assumed you could never really love her, I did my best to hide her until no one saw her anymore. I even tried to hide her scent. Slowly, without realizing, I changed and lost her. With piss elegant perfume I could scarcely afford, I changed the way I smelled to get rid of the real me, to get rid of *her*.

I recall her now only briefly in familiar smells sneaking up like cat breath, rain on dead leaves, trash fires burning in the hollows of summer. Honeysuckle embarrasses me, how I tried to remember you in the fragrant blossoms where I tried to forget the first time you attacked me.

The first time you attacked me, I sensed your anger, mistaking it for passion. When we visited the old lodge that summer night, we were meant for each other, the way our bodies kept turning in the bed and fitting into each other, the rhythms of our breathing falling in sync. I tasted the intimate fragrance of you.

Breathing your musk, sniffing your body, smelling your beery breath as we were falling asleep, I had never done that. I loved the way you smelled, your breath, your sweat. I couldn't quit breathing you into me.

Consensual

Consensual is a strange word that sounds like the name of an expensive perfume sold to women and girls, an expensive perfume that goes off in the heat and gets strange.

I couldn't quit inhaling you like a drug. I took you deep inside my lungs, savoring every odor. Wanting to give myself to you, I was grateful that I didn't think it would be this way. Instead of an engagement ring, you gave me imprints of hands across my neck, bruises the color of the night in the shape of your fingers. Like the ghosts of who we were, who I was and will never be, the river stinking of fish and rot and moss and leaves traveled toward a love so fierce it marked me during the incident caught on video surveillance. Those poor-quality images.

The Tangled Woman

The trickle of melt water tinkling was funereal music for a woman tangled in the branches of a tree. The death of the tangled woman, who had become lost in the storm while running from her husband in the blizzard, was a lesson to look for the lost in places most don't consider searching.

Whenever I hear of women and girls gone missing from their lives, I look where others don't consider searching, inside the cages of rebuilt iron staircases, beneath panels of vaulted ceilings, in forgotten cellars, even in trash bins. I hope others will do the same to discover me among lost women. Pay no attention to the shadow flickering in the blue curtains of the window in the reflection of what's behind you in the long mirror. If it frightens you, don't look into the mirror.

Gazing into the mirror on the night I was attacked, I saw the reflection of what was behind me. I smelled a strange scent as I hid. Down the hall, around the corner, an orange lamp glowed red in the dark. Like the long blue curtains, a shadow hovered. I spent the last moments of my life tangled in my own fear though I did nothing wrong, nothing to deserve this.

Terror, the Perfume

Terror, the perfume of petrified women and traumatized girls, releases a chemical signature of pheromones unconsciously detected during fight-or-flight.

The Coveted Scent That Whispers:

She Wanted It.

Voice Over Documentary:

A Confessional Narrative of a Perfumer

(her face hidden in shadow)

I've smelled Terror on my body and on the bodies of
other women.

As a girl, I first sniffed it on my skin whenever men followed,
leering.

Once I saved enough money, I bought piss-elegant perfume I
could scarcely afford.

It changed the way I smelled to get rid of the real me.

FRAGRANCE PYRAMID

EVAPORATION DURATION (MINUTES)

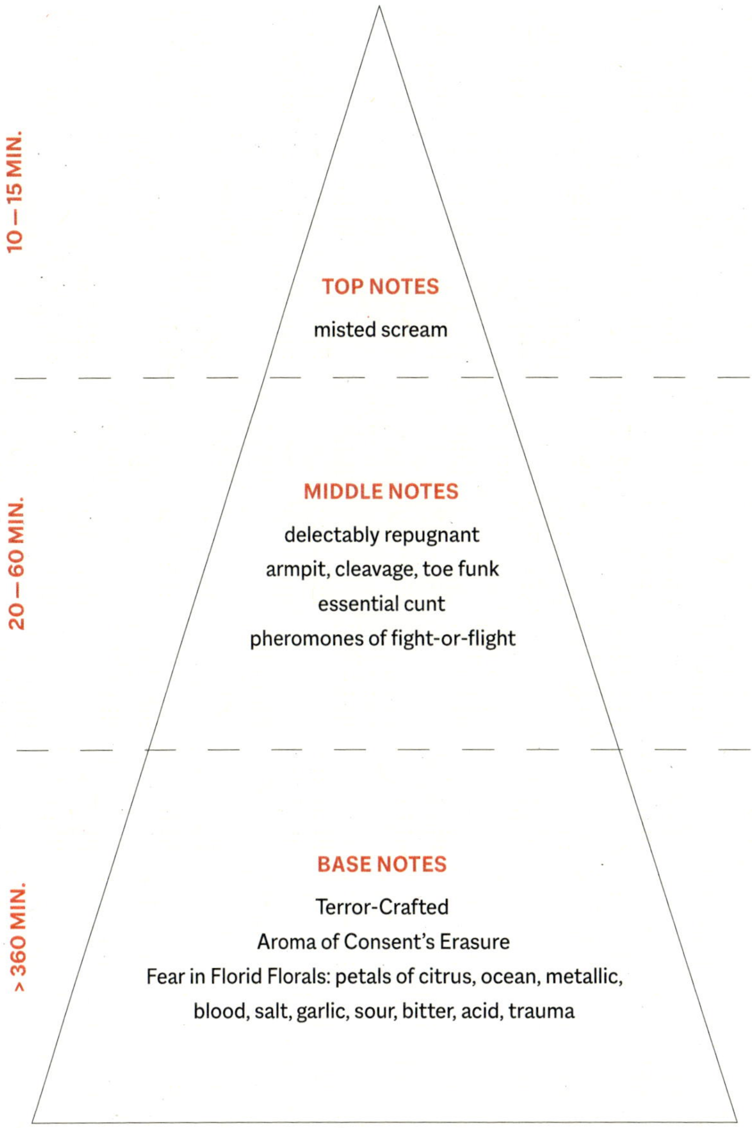

10 — 15 MIN.

TOP NOTES

misted scream

20 — 60 MIN.

MIDDLE NOTES

delectably repugnant
armpit, cleavage, toe funk
essential cunt
pheromones of fight-or-flight

> 360 MIN.

BASE NOTES

Terror-Crafted
Aroma of Consent's Erasure
Fear in Florid Florals: petals of citrus, ocean, metallic,
blood, salt, garlic, sour, bitter, acid, trauma

RISK OF THEFT

-EVIDENCE-

FILE NO. Exhibit 16

NAME Armed with Orchids

SECTIONS Funerals for the Living; Hypothetical Orchids; The Never Taxi; Be Creative

Funerals for the Living

No driver would allow the injured woman into his taxi after midnight, so I drove her to safety after her boyfriend had thrown her against an antique bathtub, knocking her head repeatedly on the cast iron walls. Because she didn't know how long she had been out or where her boyfriend had gone, I stayed with her.

That's how I got this blood in my car, how it became a Never Taxi, picking up customers no taxi service would – murdered women who hadn't died yet. They were on a journey toward death, though they didn't know it.

At the precinct, the police did everything right, took the bleeding woman to the hospital, put out a warrant for the boyfriend, and invited a battered women's advocate. In the hospital waiting room, I would have stayed, but the bleeding woman asked me to go inside the recovery room.

"She had been unconscious in that bathtub for how long?" The nurses kept saying.

I didn't know because she didn't know. There was no way of knowing unless the boyfriend knew, and he probably would never tell. The woman was shaking, couldn't hold a cup of water, spilling it over the table. I held the cup to her lips. She gulped, coughing water in my eyes. When she asked for more water, I fetched it.

Filling the cup at the water fountain in the hall, I overheard the woman tell the advocate that she had changed her mind, asking the advocate to inform the police that she no longer wanted to press charges because she loved her boyfriend, who was often kind to her. The advocate told the woman to hire a florist to arrange the flowers for her funeral.

Hypothetical Orchids

In florist school, I had arranged flowers for hypothetical funerals. I was assigned Sharon Tate. She was my first real teacher. I have studied photographs of the rope looped around her neck. I'm stronger for it now, though I've only seen the photographs in black and white. Covered in blood, she was eight months pregnant, stabbed to death. Her face stayed with me. There was no horror there, no peace. For Sharon and her child, I chose a delicate whisper of double white orchids, a wordless message to distract from the truth: Murder demands a floral response. Petals soften the blow. I've seen a lot of ghosts since then, including my own, but nothing prepared me for encountering the woman who emerged from her coffin. She was still alive and deeply in love with her murderer when she hired me to arrange the gardenias for her funeral. Since her death hadn't happened yet, I couldn't erase it with flowers, though I've prepared myself for the worst by looking at crime scene photos, so I could never be shocked by her passing.

The Never Taxi

Just after sunrise, I entered my house to rest after a long night. I was startled awake when a woman with broken arms used her head to knock on the door of my home. When I opened the door, she said to me, "This is my dream house. I'll be safe here."

I asked her to repeat what she had said, and she said, "You're living in my dream house. Is this your dream house, too?"

"No," I told her. "It's just my house."

"Not anymore," she said. "This is my dream house, and you're in my dream. Get out. Now. Understand?"

I understood all too well. There was no arguing with a woman with broken arms. I knew it was pointless to pack up my things. I was homeless in her dream where my house and everything in it was no longer mine. I left. She moved in.

I would have to start dreaming about a house that wasn't mine and then find that house in my dream to evict the person living inside, or else I would be homeless forever. It took me a while, quite a long time, to dream my dream house and then to find it in my dream. The only problem was, when I knocked on the door, a woman with broken legs answered, struggling on crutches. Her family was living inside my dream house, including her sister with the broken jaw, her daughter with broken ribs, and her aunt with a broken neck. I didn't want to do to them what had been done to me, so I walked away from my dream house and pretended it wasn't mine.

Be Creative

My roommates and I have installed a Segal lock and chain locks. We change the locks and keep the doors and windows barred because my murderer walks the roof next door to look down into our windows.

The landlord says the bars over the windows are a fire hazard and we must have them removed, so my roommates and I go around boobytrapping the windows with bells and bottles, until we get the idea to use razor blades, tacks, nails, and knives.

"Be creative," we say, but I've already called another florist to arrange the flowers for my funeral: blue irises and blood roses, their dark red, almost black, stems coated with thin, sharp prickles, their strong metallic scent akin to the scent of blood.

We have blood-rose nightlights burning, never in the iris-blue rooms where we are sleeping. We thread locks inside certain doors. When we hear my murderer breaking in, we call out in our deepest voices to say we are armed with orchids. We barricade the doors as he picks the locks. If his fingers slip through, we hand him a snowy gardenia and release our dog, Delphinium.

-EVIDENCE-

FILE NO. Exhibit 17

NAME Murder Ballads

SECTIONS Kindness Among the Looted Bodies; Murder Ballads

NO HUMMING WHILE READING

Kindness Among the Looted Bodies

The hawk as it returns to its nest, mushrooms growing in fallen leaves, trees along the lakeshore, songs of every last moment echoed you turning sixteen and dressing your dog like a lion in the golden leaves of autumn.

Among children biking through neighborhood streets, you were lost. Men rode horses into fields to find you the autumn you disappeared to fall in what I dreamed was love.

You fell in love with the fiddler who spoke to you through music.

In Louisiana, his ballads, ever changing as sky before a storm, swept you into two-steps with his friends and brothers, his sisters who became your sisters, knowing the ways of folk musicians. In songs they loved each other. Their songs became a part of you, a name woven into echoes along the water after floods.

Rain changes everything in the golden light of old mansions where people aren't supposed to go unless they are invited to cook, clean, or sing for the rich. Even as a child, you understood why people like us, who had no money, danced in rain.

At night, you are lost. I dream you dancing.

I dream you falling into the fiddler's welcoming arms.

I dream you into his music as rain falls over forests of melody.

Lyrics in his eyes, the rivers and the railyards, the paddle wheel inside you complaining about the men always asking him to play Black Betty because his sisters are tired of singing, tired of you asking why the whip in southern prisons used to torture men is a woman.

Amazing Grace was also a woman, his mother's name, Grace, the thing that will save us from ourselves as we worry for you, attempting to understand if lost means forever.

When we found the opossum stranded in a tree after the flood, the land had become water. The fiddle player paddled his boat to the opossum and climbed the tree to help the opossum down only for you to watch in silence, then in cheering, as the opossum scrambled away from him and back up the tree.

Some stranded people are like the opossum in the tree. They don't want to be saved, even when their world is gone; they don't want a stranger coming to grab them from their last anchor. They hold. But some are like me, waiting for the stranger. I never knew until he sang a song about a woman who walked into the water to enter her flooded house, to find the rooms where her husband and child had drowned to be with them again. Glimpsing her face reflected in the water, the woman swam the flooded streets, knowing she could never go back.

If all bodies are looted by death, some of us have our bodies looted when we are still alive.

I've spent days and nights searching for you before spending years searching for your body.

The fiddler's sisters sing about a funeral home where a lonely undertaker lovingly caresses the bodies of dead women. The necrophiliac could never caress the living, and I wonder why, why is it so hard for people to see each other and know each other when they are needing each other, why a living woman creates fear and revulsion in some men thrilled by the bodies of the dead.

I try not to think of our mother's friend in college, the one our family keeps thinking of when they are terrified of what happened to you, imagining the girl who was beaten with a wooden log by a stranger who wanted to separate her from her body. He had no use for her body while she was still inside of it where she could see him with her eyes. A neighbor found her body, headless, because her killer had kept her head to wash and style her hair and put makeup on her face as if she were a doll. He killed her so he could have her head, which meant nothing to him until it was taken from her.

Because she's more than a headless woman, more than a looted body, you ask the fiddler to play a song for her. He asks her name, what she was like, where she lived, what she dreamed. He asks nothing about her head or her body or her murderer, and that's one of the reasons you fall for the fiddler. You feel her spirit soaring in his song.

Murder Ballads

Sometimes his songs flowed like the river, cutting through the forest, and sometimes you could enter the songs like the rooms of familiar houses where you lived long ago. Falling in love with the fiddle player meant strange houses became familiar in song, though you never ventured inside until he fiddled the doors open.

Just by playing the fiddle, he told you what he wanted more than he could say with words. He played for hours, which took strength and skill. He played until sweat ran down his long-wet hair on the tavern stage as if he had been drenched in rain.

Later, you would lick the sweat off his eyelids, knowing how jealous women and girls would become since he could kiss you by playing his fiddle. He could work you over without touching your body, stroking you with sound. You often wondered if it were a game he played, then you realized this was no game. He was doing it to other women.

Sometimes when he sang songs, he sang the dead alive so you knew them better than you knew the living, his sisters singing along, gazing into your eyes until you wanted to be a singer, to be some sort of musician so you could be part of their world where the dead breathed through song.

You became the rattler. The girls gave you a rattle so you could shake it, twitching into garden. Going into song with your rattle was the most exciting thing you ever did, stepping on stage with them at the barn dances like trespassing until you realized you were part of the band, dancing.

The dead danced shadows for him and for you and for the music he wanted to haunt. To join them on the road at night, as the van drove the highway, you stroked his long chestnut hair, fingers strumming his beard as he slept.

Careful, careful now, his sisters whispered with their eyes as night became morning. He needs to sleep through dawn since he works the stage into tavern light.

This is the moment you realize he trusts you enough to fall asleep in your arms and has given you the gift of loving you enough to let you cradle him even as he sleeps, to trust you to hold him sleeping as you watch his eyes darting beneath his lids while wondering if he dreams of you.

One night when he's sleeping with his head resting on your lap, his older sister tells you their mother was strangled by their father in a drunken rage. Never speak of her because they saw her die, the other sisters warn, though they speak of her at night while he sleeps until you make the mistake of reminding the older sister what was said and she claims you are mistaken. This moment becomes another forgotten memory because his murder ballads are love songs where the mother is unwritten, her face gazing through the van's dark windows.

DO NOT TURN AROUND

-EVIDENCE-

FILE NO. Exhibit 18

NAME Misdirection

SECTIONS Adult Daycare; Somewhere Under the Rainbow; A Depressive Speaks; Ozark Beauties; Family Photographs

Adult Daycare

Most of our clients are women because women typically live longer, and longevity means they have to acclimate to being the last of their cabal, united unbeknownst to those outside their disappearing group. Lone survivors of the girls of their youth, these infamous women, who once lived in the shadow of our community's celebrated men, are husbandless, nameless, voiceless. They have buried their husbands, sometimes even daughters and sons.

It's worse, I think, for the ones whose families are still alive and no longer come to visit. It happens gradually, the visits getting shorter and farther apart, tapering off to phone calls, then nothing, until it's hard to find a face with as much kindness as Kate Winslet, the grace of Dorothy Dandridge, or a woman as feisty as Jane Fonda.

For several of our clients, Bette Davis is alive and well, a frequent visitor cherished for her take-no-shit demeanor. Natalie Portman is the perfect replacement daughter, Tom Cruise the capable son-in-law, reliable like James Cagney, though no man can hold a candle to James Garner, whom some of our clients call "the only James."

Meryl Streep, all poise, graciously visits here once a week, despite her busy schedule. Cate Blanchett, unlike certain sisters replaced, never disappoints. Denzel Washington, Anthony Hopkins and Gary Oldman are so kind to us, as are Florence Pugh, Sidney Poitier, and the charmingly cool Julianne Moore.

Our best clients, most of them elderly, are serving time for crimes that should not be mentioned in polite company, crimes that have nothing to do with the law and everything to do with time because there is a fine line between living and living too long. As disappointed as they have been by the people they loved and the ones who once loved them, they have never been disappointed by Michael Caine as they have been by fathers, uncles, brothers, and sons.

Because all they do is watch movies on the televisions all day, our clients here at the adult daycare think actors are their friends. Television is better than any drug, replacing friends and family who stopped visiting long ago. The televisions are always on, playing movies with Samuel L. Jackson, Christian Bale, and Michelle Williams. If it makes our clients happy, it's okay. If it keeps them calm, it's a good thing. Not much else does.

Lena Horne, Ingrid Bergman, and Olivia Colman are very much a presence, not ghosts, but alive with us and alive to us, realer than the ghosts of families who have faded away, out of touch, too busy to call or stop by because time keeps getting the best of all of us, except for the people in the movies.

Somewhere Under the Rainbow

The screenplays we wrote bled through wounds of computer-generated women who became distractions written in blood. The diner's only customers were uncredited scriptwriters; so, we thought the studio and its actors were playing pranks, payback for the movies. What was it that investors and advertisers wanted the audience to unsee, and how did they erase it from the viewers' minds?

I never tired of the mystery of misdirection, wondering what it was that I was paid to help audiences forget.

Whenever we asked who owned the rights to actors' faces, they told us there would soon be no such thing as actors, and we began to believe them at the diner, where our servers were Johnny Depp, Brad Pitt, and Benicio Del Toro, sauntering to our table to take our order. A fresh roach twitching on his pencil, Benicio wrote: *biscuits and gravy, bacon (crispy), sausage, girts, hashbrowns, eggs sunny-side-up.*

How much to tip Queen Latifah, Charlize Theron, Pam Grier, or Marilyn Monroe? The food was damn delicious, but roaches kept diving into our coffee and gravy like Olympic swim teams.

"These roaches aren't real," my coauthor said to Rosario Dawson.

"No shit, Sherlock," Eartha Kitt whispered as Benedict Cumberbatch walked through the back door.

Whoopi Goldberg and James Dean flipped flapjacks with

Joan Crawford, smoking near burners. Other waitresses, mostly background, were more technically gifted than Oscar winners. Near Julia Roberts dishing up mac 'n' cheese across from Clark Gable wiping sugar jars, Dorothy Dandridge hummed. Charlie Chaplin, busboy, flirted with Vivien Leigh, a lousy server.

What was my writing helping to erase, and what was being erased from me as Vivien Leigh blew my co-writers a kiss where roaches procreated on dusty window blinds near Eddie Murphy's shadow?

I flirted with Lena Horne, distracting me from something I could never quite understand.

Rock Hudson winked. I winked back, then realized he was winking at Jeffrey Wright.

Will Smith smiled at Chris Rock.

Robert Redford, Clint Eastwood, Laurence Olivier, and Denzel Washington were changing shifts, counting out the cash drawer, tallying the change in the register housing a family of roaches in gleaming black drawers of scratched plastic. Little baby roaches clung to pennies as Rita Moreno and Gary Cooper argued with Jodie Foster about a steak undercooked by Tom Hanks, brushing roach eggs off hashbrowns with a butter knife to test the meat.

Robert De Niro said, "Put the brick on it!"

Gene Hackman motioned to Heath Ledger at the grill.

Katharine Hepburn called out to Robert Blake, "The damn brick is gone!"

It wasn't Bogart who Bogarted the brick. Garbo had dropped it into her handbag after using it to crush the largest roach I had ever seen, a roach so large I'm not even sure it was a roach. Its face was Vincent Price's face. Garbo kept looking at the brick after she mashed it on the painted cinderblock, as if she needed to show it to save it for later.

The dishwasher, Marlon Brando, kept signaling to Viola Davis to steal the brick out of Garbo's handbag. Taking a smoke break, Viola gossiped with Cate Blanchett. Montgomery Clift served me a roach burger with a generous side of mayo glistening like the reflection of the moon on the motel pool where Valentino swam with John Travolta. Elizabeth Taylor asked if everything was to our satisfaction, ignoring scuttling in the shadow beneath us.

Roaches glistened like amber jewels over Audrey Hepburn's delicate hands when Samuel L. Jackson kissed her quickly on the neck. Unflinching as roaches walked her slender fingers like suicide bridges, Halle Berry refilled saltshakers with Julie Andrews, whose earrings were nymphs emerging from ootheca. That took a certain nerve to emerge and keep emerging, a gumption, as my grandma would say, that is, if she could speak upon seeing our busboy, Cary Grant, flicking a long, dark antenna as if adjusting a curl over his eye.

A flying roach landed on Barbara Stanwyck's cheek, and Jack Nicholson leaned in for a kiss to blow the roach into the soda machine. Looking right at the wings twitching, I noted the lamplight gleaming off those amber wings.

Bette Davis smirked, cigarette in mouth, a roach falling with her ash as a teenage Judy Garland approached with a fresh pot of coffee. Gingerly, Judy refilled my steaming cup of roach coffee. After filling my cup to the brim, she waited for me to taste it, a roach leg floating to the surface. I took an appreciative sip, thankful she was a young girl again, Dorothy with roaches instead of rainbows.

A Depressive Speaks

When the sky is bluer than Paul Newman's eyes and men working toll booths on the bridge are as affable as Adam West, wake me up. When birds are singing sweeter than Billie Holiday, when the waves are rippling more gracefully than Maria Tallchief and the winds are flying higher than Christopher Reeve in his red cape, stir me. When the leaves on the oak trees are sparkling lighter than Twiggy and the river is flowing into velvet meadows as mysterious as Vincent Price, don't let me sleep. When the traffic on the highway is moving faster than Houdini freeing himself from underwater chains and the radio is playing a song as big as Fats Domino's dream, get me out of bed. When the air is as fresh and clean as Rosemary Clooney's house and every stranger walking down the street is as kind and polite as Jimmy Stewart, tell me it's time. When people are feeling as good as Nina Simone and couples are dancing in time as precisely as John Travolta, wake me up.

Ozark Beauties

Love letters written in blood, ruined panties wrapped in old t-shirts, I ran with kids on the Delta, long before I thought my life was ending because I was pregnant. I started jumping off the stairs, leaping off porch rails. Falling to grasses, I shivered. Bleeding beside the strawberry patch's Ozark Beauties, I pretended my blood was strawberries.

Family Photographs

Here is my gift to you: a photograph of your father throwing a baby into the ocean to teach it how to swim. That baby grew up to be a lifeguard. In this next photograph, your older brother is making rabbit ears behind your father's head. Even though he's smiling, your father's eyes are not smiling, as if he knows. Here is a photograph of caked mascara running down your sister's face when your father compares her to an aging beauty queen in old photographs by cutting-and-pasting your mother's face onto her face. Never mind. What I really want to know is why do we smile in photographs? Mother taught me and my sister to do that in our childhood, shamed us if we didn't smile for the camera, because those who don't smile ruin the photograph. I'm still broken by photographs of us smiling at strangers who don't know how to love us. Because it hurts to see these photographs of our family, I take a photograph of you standing in front of the brightly lit window.

MAY CAUSE STRONG FLAS

-EVIDENCE-

FILE NO. Exhibit 19

NAME Remember Me

SECTIONS Remember Me

Remember Me

In the psychiatric unit, I keep asking to speak to you, and the nurse keeps telling me that you are no longer alive. I keep asking to speak to my sister, and the nurse tells me that I don't have a sister, I never had a sister, and I should stop asking to speak to my sister. I ask to speak to my brother. I ask to speak to my father. The nurse tells me my father was just here yesterday and I refused to speak to him. *Remember? There's your father. That man over there. See him? In the corner, he's waiting to talk to you.* When I see him, I ask to speak to you, and he tells me you are no longer alive. I keep asking to speak to my sister, and he tells me slowly, calmly, I don't have a sister, I never had a sister, and I should stop asking to speak to my sister. I ask to speak to my brother. I ask to speak to my father. The man tells me he is my father. I ask him to speak to you. He keeps telling me that you are no longer alive until I ask to speak to my brother. The nurse tells me that my brother was here two days ago, and I refused to speak to him because of what he was telling me about you. *Your brother will be here tomorrow,* she says. Now is tomorrow. *There's your brother. That man over there? See him? Go to him.* Waiting in the hall, he's ready to talk to me. When I ask to speak to you, he says the police never found you inside the rustic bedroom where we're young and poor, holding each other in the dark, our nakedness illuminated by moonlight.

A pond stretching over soft green grasses, where in mossy water we swim with children whose faces resemble our own. A window over the kitchen sink overlooking the woods like a fairytale, beyond the woods and the frozen pond, the snow of distant mountains edging sky in the psychiatric unit, where you keep asking to speak to your mother, and the nurse keeps telling you your mother is no longer alive. You keep asking to speak to your sister, and the nurse tells you that you don't have a sister, you never had a sister, you should stop asking to speak to your sister. You ask to speak to your brother. You ask to speak to your father. The nurse tells you that your father was just here yesterday and you refused to speak to him. *Remember? There's your father. That man over there. See him?* In the corner, he's waiting to talk to you. When you see him, you ask to speak to your mother, and he tells you that your mother is no longer alive. You keep asking to speak to your sister, and he tells you slowly, calmly, you don't have a sister, you never had a sister, and you should stop asking to speak to your sister. You ask to speak to your brother. You ask to speak to your father. The man tells you that he is your father. You ask him to speak to your mother. He keeps telling you that your mother is no longer alive until you ask to speak to your brother. The nurse tells you that your brother was here two days ago and you refused to speak to him because of what he was telling you about your father. *Your brother will be here tomorrow*, she says. Now is tomorrow. *There's your brother. That man over there. See him? Go to him.* Waiting in the hall, he's ready to talk to you. When you ask to speak to your father, your brother says your father has been telling lies about our first pets, two terriers, basking in the glow of hearth light, near a window framing misty morning.

In the mist called time, a grandfather clock with a large golden pendulum and heavy gleaming weights, the faces of the sun and the moon, the stars and the planets, moving with the clock's hands. Through the mist, I see great-grandmother's day, when our family's houses were built to last, the pine floors women swept, hewn by the callused hands of fathers. Men had rough hands from building cradles and coffins. After a house was built, keeping the inside clean was women's work. Women had to keep house or else the house would go away. In order for a girl to become a woman, she had to learn of the body and its mysteries by caring for the sick in the sickroom and the pregnant in rooms of waiting. She nursed the newly born and the dying. Girls were trained to wash linens and to wash bodies, to sew curtains, to cook, to make beds and to scrub and polish and dust and varnish. Boys went with men to work fields. Their dreams scattered like cottonwood seeds in summer.

Staring at the cottonwood seeds drifting outside the windows of the psychiatric unit, she keeps asking to speak to her father about the year of our wedding, the house we bought with borrowed money, and the doctor keeps telling her that her father is no longer alive. She keeps asking to speak to her sister, and the nurse tells her that she doesn't have a sister, she never had a sister, she should stop asking to speak to her sister. She asks to speak to her brother. She asks to speak to her father. The nurse tells her that her father was just here yesterday, and she refused to speak to him. Remember? There's her father. That man over there. See him? In the corner, he's waiting to talk to her. When she sees him, she asks to speak to her father, and he tells her that her father is no longer alive. She keeps asking to speak to her sister, and he tells her slowly, calmly, *You don't have a sister, you never had a sister, and you should stop asking to speak to your sister.* She asks to speak to her brother. She asks to speak to her father. The man tells her that he is her father. She asks him to speak to her brother. He keeps telling her that her brother is no longer alive until she asks to speak to her father. The nurse tells her that her brother was here two days ago and she refused to speak to him because of what he was telling her about her father. *Your brother will be here tomorrow,* she says. Now is tomorrow. There's her brother. That man over there. *Go to him, waiting in the hall.* When she asks to speak to her father, he says, *See him?*

After the riot in the violent ward, she is one of the shirtless women rejoicing bullet holes into an American flag because they have realized there never was an America like the

America that they were taught to believe in. When they visited the graves of soldiers to understand why, their grandmothers said it was impolite and unamerican to mention girls who didn't know their fathers were shadows.

In the shadow of her father, the shadow of her mother keeps asking to speak to his sister, and the nurse keeps telling them his sister is no longer alive. Her father keeps asking to speak to his sister, and the nurse tells him that he doesn't have a sister, he never had a sister, he should stop asking to speak to his sister. He asks to speak to his brother. He asks to speak to his father. The nurse tells him his father was just here yesterday and he refused to speak to him. *Remember? There's your father. That man over there. See him? In the corner, he's waiting to talk to you.* When he sees him, he asks to speak to his sister, and the man tells him his sister is no longer alive. He keeps asking to speak to his sister, and the nurses tell him slowly, calmly, he doesn't have a sister, he never had a sister, and he should stop asking to speak to his sister. He asks to speak to his brother. He asks to speak to his father. The man tells him that he is his father. He asks the man to speak to his sister. The man keeps telling him that his sister is no longer alive until he asks to speak to his brother. The nurse tells him that his brother was here two days ago and he refused to speak to him because of what his brother was telling him about his sister. *Your brother will be here tomorrow,* she says.

Now is tomorrow. *There's your brother. That man over there. See him? Go to him.* Waiting in the hall, he's ready to talk to you. When he asks to speak to his sister, his brother says, *Remember me.*

WASH HANDS FIRST

-EVIDENCE-

FILE NO. Exhibit 20

NAME Traumatized Sons

SECTIONS Ocean Eyes; Mrs. Davidson; Mrs. Davidson's Baby

Ocean Eyes

1) *The Sinking Son*

Yachts go down into depths where my beloved son sinks. His congested ears popping on descent, watery fluid invades his stomach with immersion to an underwater forest of aerial roots. Dunes cradle bones in black puddles like congealed blood where sea creatures devour webs of hair.

2) *The Drowning*

Another young man has been found in the water. Ask the police on the shore if it's just another unexplained drowning. Ask the sheriff. Ask the pathologist, the harbor fire department, and the medical examiner. Night falls on the coast, and another body is floating. As investigators turn the body toward the sky, don't gaze into the eyes of the drowned. Have you ever wondered about the expression "drowning eyes"? Froth plumes around his mouth and nostrils. His distended lungs and airways swell with debris. Like blood spots on a slide, red starfish bloom in aneurysm.

3) *Gloved Hands*

The coroner examines the young man's remains in the morgue's harsh light. Syphoning the lungs' aspirated liquid, strangers meet in private autopsy. Gloved hands swim halogen lights flooding the steel table. The medical examiner holds the fragile fingers of the deceased's left hand. Searching for sediment and froth in the trachea, the medical examiner is gentle like a caring mother, a soft touch like tides manipulating stilling fingers reaching rigor mortis. Delicate twists of lividity trace postmortem injury and impersonal ravages of shoreline. Cold water that once refrigerated the dead man's body, slowing decomposition, makes pinpointing his time of death as difficult as capturing the moon with a lure dropped into black water.

4) *The "Washerwoman Change"*

Examining the maceration of skin, the family doctor is as attentive as a lover, eyes dancing over the whitening, the thickening, the wrinkling, epidermis integrity lost with time. His gloved fingers drift to the drowned man's left hand, so fragile that to touch the hand is to deglove it as it reaches for beaches, bays, kelp forests. Pathology encountered during autopsy: the loneliness, the hopelessness, the noting of the misogynistically named "washerwoman change" in the softening hands. The mushy folds of his fingers and palm in slippage are deemed womanly: *washer-womanly.* This medical tradition, common terminology, is scientific autopsy talk, but also passive, unconscious, imagistic woman hating in the innocent misgendering of a dead man's hands. All too often, to drown as a man is to have a washerwoman's hands, so is to drown as a woman or a child. Drowned hands are hands of the washerwoman, who couldn't afford to buy oceanfront property.

5) *Drowning Eyes*

The unfortunate investigator gazes into the eyes of the drowned. His gaze, coastward, seems to be searching for sloping dunes, whales, sealion children, eagles flying above a white gull swooping in formation like wind-whipped bridal veils floating waves of firmament. On the horizon, the sky is the ghost of the water until nightfall when the water becomes the ghost of the sky.

Mrs. Davidson

After carefully bathing her two-week old son in the kitchen sink, Mrs. Davidson laid him down on the breadboard and hacked off his head and arms. After wiping the blood off her hands, Mrs. Davidson asked me to drive her to the supermarket because she wanted to shop for milk and ice cream.

Mrs. Davidson's Baby

My mother's star was lost in the sky. In a brightness she could never see shining on us, her faith vanished in postpartum depression, where she thought wisdom was wasted on wise men, just as nails were wasted on the cross. Little did she know, her knives flashed brilliantly like the stars I would travel to. I had lived many lives and would live again after she killed me. When Jesus was a child, I was also a child, wondering if anything could end this vicious cycle. Because death could not snuff us out, Mother thought her life ended with mine, but my life never ended because I was part of eternity. When Confucius was a child, I was also a child, wondering why we couldn't buy happiness if we must pay the price. Mother made her sacrifice because she thought nothing has beauty if I could see it.

-EVIDENCE-

FILE NO. Exhibit 21

NAME Almost Heavenly Babies

SECTIONS You Sound Drunk, You Probably Shouldn't Leave the House Today; Don't Ask Me Why; River Girl and Delta Queen; Almost Heavenly Babies

HOLD CLOSELY - NO HARSH LIGHT

You Sound Drunk, You Probably Shouldn't Leave the House Today

We never speak of the reasons for her drinking, though her husband was in the Navy overseas, a high-ranking officer, leaving her alone at home. When I was a child, whenever her husband was away, my neighbor would visit my mother, stumbling into our house, reeking of whiskey and crying about her husband, not wanting to be alone at night. She was the type of woman other women called a doll. Pretty, slender, elfin-faced with no children, she was youthful and kind with an aura of fragile, feminine innocence nurtured like a pet in a well-swept house with caramel aluminum siding and wooden shutters painted sunny-sky blue. A divorced woman also abandoned by a man, my mother felt sorry for our neighbor and asked me to stay over with her to keep her company, since my mother had to watch my baby sisters and had work in the early morning as a secretary at the meat-packing plant. I packed my tattered overnight bag and skipped over to the neighbor's neatly decorated house, where I slept in crisply laundered paisley bedsheets in her husband's place as she attempted to fall into a drunken sleep, shivering, curled against my back, spooning me. Sensing her dreaming, I woke in the dark with her hands on me. I was thirteen when it started, fifteen when it ended with her fingers creeping inside me. I pretended to sleep. At sunrise, she cooked me a breakfast of burnt buttered toast dusted in cinnamon sugar while warning me about men. She watched me eat as she sucked her fingers while sipping bourbon-spiked tea.

Don't Ask Me Why

While my best friend Kristy was starving herself in college, I found my dreams in a donut hole. As Kristy slowly faded away from malnourishment, I found hope in a pocket of cherry pie, that place where the filling missed the crust, not quite air, not entirely empty, sweet bubble bursting on my tongue. After Kristy weighed herself after eating a cup of bone broth and felt guilty for having the broth, she would skip rope for an hour before sleeping that night as I found the truth baked between the layers of a flaky buttermilk biscuit, my life purpose in a turnover turning, meaning tucked inside a savory fritter frittering my time away. I was fat, and Kristy was thin. Kristy was a Barbie without breasts, and I was Rubenesque. A well-meaning boyfriend had advised me to "familiarize myself" with the Flemish painter Peter Paul Rubens, who often painted women with large, fat bodies. Kristy and I were the best of friends, though she was so afraid of becoming full-figured that she refused to eat, to avoid being like me, though she loved me. That was all that mattered, all anyone else could ever see until she was admitted to the hospital and was told she would be force fed through a tube if she didn't start to eat. She wept, and the doctor threatened her. Her parents pleaded with her and asked me to convince her to take a single bite. She smiled warily. Still, she refused food, didn't want anything to do with it because she was afraid of being fat like me. Though she was too weak for her heart to make it through the night and was being tube fed, nurses tried to save her while I was in the bakery near the hospital eating donuts straight from the box. Stuffing my face with dingdongs, I was worrying about Kristy, how I would ever live without her, when a woman I didn't know walked up to me and asked why I was letting myself go.

River Girl and Delta Queen

Mississippi sky like a watercolor sundown, River Girl finds me, her Delta Queen, in the wake of frothy river water. Like an elk jumping over rocks, she leaps from stable to garage to barn to my arms in the trailer park. Some people who live here are secret millionaires, men say. I'm going to marry one someday. Other people live with a million secrets like my friend Kamba and me. We never told anyone about the man who asked to use our phone on one of the nights when our mothers went out dancing. Alone in the trailer, we let him in our house to help him, though we knew better and were not allowed to open the door to strangers. He pulled a gun on us in the kitchen. He jostled Kamba in a headlock and then shoved her into the closet. On the kitchen floor, he tackled me, then he tugged Kamba out of the closet and he put us both in a headlock and then threw me in the closet, before throttling her in the living room. He went on like that, taking turns choking us, stripping us, controlling us, slapping us, biting us, outraging us, strangling us, while tearing through every room of the trailer house, until he was exhausted. After he left, we stumbled about the trailer while cleaning up the evidence in every room. Before our moms returned, we were ashamedly mopping up our blood, our secrets, and our urine with vinegar, bleach, tea tree oil, tears, and dish soap, as if the crime were ours. Even now, as women, we're still certain we will be blamed if our mothers find out.

Almost Heavenly Babies

If you've ever gone to an amusement park without being amused, you know certain places are full of lies meant to keep rubes happy. In a pageant of big mechanical toys, lines move slowly for rides that go too fast. On the road to the park, a woman named Mary Miller sells handmade objects called Heavenly Babies in her unauthorized roadside stand. Mary comes from a long line of ancestors who were dollmakers of Nuremberg, goosewomen carving wheeled horses, later recreated life sized at the entrance for Pinocchio's Tunnel, that little dark place where I couldn't help remembering my uncle, who disappeared from prison after seven years of solitary confinement. Raised in poverty as a child, he grew into a man who always carried large sums of money, bundles of crisp bills he called "cheese." One of millions disappearing with him every year into oblivion, that slippery category of the missing where headlines are clickbait catacombs, his illegitimate child, a delinquent, was kept in a Catholic home for neglected boys, his name appearing in droves of obscene letters. Whoever George was to the letter writer before disappearing, after coming back to us, he grew into a man devoted to justice, working for the law to catch the killer at the amusement park. "Heavenly Babies" was the amusement-park killer's name for his victims, and that name gave Mary Miller an idea of what to call her creations, which she sold outside the very park where the attacks happened. The killer was a curious type of rapist, who only wanted to assault women who were with men — boyfriends and girlfriends, husbands and wives, brothers and sisters, fathers and daughters. For a long time, I wondered why he chose couples, why he killed the man but let the woman live, then my grandmother explained it to me. Women were considered property of men in her day, and the Heavenly Babies killer wasn't just motivated by sex but by the old-fashioned notion of stealing another man's property. Intending to take a woman from a man, he robbed even me, but when I was attacked at the amusement park, it was different. I was with my friend, another girl who was mistaken for a boy because of her short hair. Almost Heavenly Babies, we were forced to do things to each other at gunpoint until he realized I wasn't her property.

THE BODY OF THIS TEXT IS ALIVE

-EVIDENCE-

FILE NO. Exhibit 22

NAME Cotard's Delusion: Walking Corpse Syndrom

SECTIONS "A Woman & a Girl Named Jane," a short play; Hurry Jane; Honeycombed with Strangers; The Story of Jane; Painted Ladies; Games; Boys; Who Are You?; Why We Never Use the Front Door; Haight Street Girls; The Prettiest Lost Girl in the City

A Woman and a Girl Named Jane

(a short play)

Woman When I was young, just a girl, I worked at a newspaper. My editor kept asking if he could give me a ride home. I let him drive me home, but he didn't drive me to my apartment. He took me to a house with an enclosure in the basement, an antique circus cage large enough to hold a tiger. He shoved me through the open door of the cage, and then he closed the door in my face, locking it. At first, I thought it was a joke, that he was pranking me and playing games, but it was no joke.

Jane The woman kissed me.
Why?
Her tongue parted my lips.
I couldn't stop wondering about the cage and her kisses.

Woman A wall of gleaming mirrors behind the cage allowed me to watch myself behind the bars.
The cage held a large perch for me to swing on.
Of ornate construction, the perch's bejeweled bar, accented in gold, glinted in the basement light.
I swung, staring into the mirror while swooping past hoops and chains and brass tops of candy-apple red.

Jane Mother thought I might learn things from the woman, but the things I learned were not the things Mother thought I was learning.
Imagine my swinging on the perch inside the intricate metal cage.
"A kiss for your thoughts," the woman whispered.
I was in love.
I can still feel her gazing into my eyes while untangling my long hair, combing me with manicured fingernails on her sleigh bed.
"What was it like?" I whispered.

Woman You might not want to know if I told you about the cage and what happened to me there. When you get to know how I was treated, really know, you won't want to. Certain things happened to make me unlike other women. These things might disgust you.

Jane I thought the woman was teasing.

Woman Ask me anything.

Jane What was it like?

Woman It seems interesting, but it wasn't. There were two big problems. One of the problems was boredom. I was usually alone. The other problem? I don't want to talk about it, but it was something that happened briefly. In some ways, boredom was the worst problem because it happened all the time when I wasn't dealing with the other problem.

Jane I don't understand.

Woman Imagine me as a girl at eighteen — skinny, impoverished, shy, afraid to look anyone in the eye, quiet, hardworking, grateful for any opportunity for professional advancement. Me, before it happened, before I went into the cage and my editor locked the door behind me.

Jane Imagine the woman.
The eldest daughter from a family of many daughters and sons, well-read but only educated in typing school, she moves from the small town that is her hometown to a town where she knows no one for a job as a typist at a newspaper. This is her first job, her first time living away from family. She lives in a tiny apartment, alone with her little dog. It's the only

place she can afford. She can't even afford a phone and has so few acquaintances in the new town where she works that if she goes missing only her editor and her dog notice.
There, there! In your imagination! Do you see that little thing in the window?
That's her little dog looking out at the street the girl typically takes home from the bus stop. Looking out the window, the little dog is waiting for the girl, who will become the woman. The dog waits and waits, looking out the window at night. As the night becomes morning, the little dog keeps waiting. The dog waits at that window from that day into the next night. It never stops.

Woman See my eyes gazing through the iron bars into my editor's eyes?

Jane No. Not me! Not me.

Woman When the girl is trapped in the cage, no matter what anyone does to her, she doesn't feel it because all she can think about is the little dog waiting at the window. The little dog must be so sad, wondering where she is. She worries it must be thirsty, hungry, lonely, terrified, thinking she has abandoned it. When she's in the cage, all she can think about is the dog, how many days it can live without her.

Jane "This dog?" I stare at the dog's bright eyes in the photograph over the sleigh bed while imagining the dog staring out the window, waiting for her.

Woman Yes.

My editor had no idea what I was really thinking. Anything he told me to do, I would do it, trying to keep track of the days, imagining my dog, how much water was left in the bowl, how much food.

Jane I imagined her dog drinking from the toilet and finding a way to open a kitchen cabinet to remove a bag of dog food.

Woman My editor's guests were couples, husbands and wives. One was my doctor. Her husband, the gym teacher, was with her. Another guest worked at the bank where I had just opened an account. He was there with his wife, the homemaker. Another group included the old married couple who delivered sandwiches to the newspaper office. I recognized some of the others, but it took me a while to place their faces. I recognized my landlord and his wife.

Jane If only her dog could find the biscuits from the cabinet and drink water from the toilet?

Woman Here, dear. These are the best! Eat one. Eat several. There are more boxes where these came from because I never denied myself anything since when I got out of that cage. I told myself I would set myself free every minute of every day.
Taste one, taste them all.
Nibble a chocolate fan.
Shove an entire chocolate into your greedy mouth.

Jane They thought they were controlling her, but they only had her body in the cage. They didn't have her mind.

Woman Who do you think was suffering more — me or my dog?
Whom do you feel the sorriest for — me or my dog?
Don't bother answering.

Jane I sat in silence, waiting, thinking: Maybe, with any luck, her dog could survive, if it didn't eat the biscuits all at once?

Woman I escaped the cage the way a tiger would escape if a man opening the door got his face too close to the tiger.

Jane I prayed for her dog, that it hadn't eaten the biscuits too quickly, that it had drank water from the toilet, that the water in the toilet was good enough to drink for more than a week.

Woman At my apartment, I found the key hidden in a false stone near the door. Unlocking the door, I heard barking! I threw open the door, weeping with delight. Imagine my joy in finding my little dog waiting for me. I held my dog and kissed it, loved it, touching its wet, cold nose to mine.

After licking my face, my dog started barking and whining. I placed it gently on the rug and it began running circles around me, rolling over onto the hardwoods to show me its belly.

Jane Everything turned out so well.

Woman My apartment was too clean. My dog had been fed, its food bowl full of fresh food, its water bowl full of fresh water.

Jane What's wrong with that?

Woman My captors had been taking care of my dog because its life was worth more than mine and they knew that the story of what happened would never be believed if I ever told it.

Jane Believing her story and taking it deep inside me, I kissed the woman while imagining I was kissing the girl in the cage. Closing my eyes, I kissed the woman more softly, realizing I was the girl in the cage.

Hurry Jane

"Hurry Jane," they say, and I wonder how many customs agents it will take to steal you from me. When the rain falls, you scream like wild dogs in the night, something breaks inside the crate, and I become frightened of what I've become. Smugglers move the tarp from the crate to show me your eyes. I want you. I begin to wonder why. They drag me away from you because it's going to take time to stop your crying. In another cage, your mother listens for your cries but hears only echoes of some poachers' hushed conversations.

Arriving on the 2:30 flight, restless women wanting company ask me, "Where can I buy a baby gorilla? How much does a chimp cost? How much does a lion cost? How much is a finger monkey?"

In Africa, gorillas are disappearing, but this makes me value you even more. You're a baby, though you'll grow to be over 400 pounds and will one day be stronger than six of me. If you live to be over sixty years old, who will change our diapers?

Seeing you, touching you, holding you inside my vintage leather jacket, none of it matters, though you were born to Kilimanjaro and the Serengeti. When you gaze at me, it's like I hear long forgotten words. When your little hand reaches for my finger, I feel an ancient melody.

Just when I think you're lost, an old man stops me along the way to the ATM to say, "Hurry to the crate. She's waiting for you."

Demanding bribes, customs officers are trying to tell me I came to Africa to do the things I never have. They say there's time to do the things they've never done, but it's going to cost more money than I've paid. They say rhinos are disappearing. They say I can potty train a monkey and eat tiger soup. They say a pet ape might outlive me and my ability to care for it. They say tiger-eye soup can make me see visions. They say eating a rhino's horn can make me stronger. They say hurry, hurry, the little one's waiting.

I must hurry to pay for you and drug you, to hide you beneath my arm and inside the secret flap sewn into my leather jacket. I have to hurry through customs, so you don't smother in my jacket, before people try to drag me away from you the way I dragged you away from your mother.

Honeycombed with Strangers

No one understands forgotten elevators like I do. They are tunnels and death traps for girls being chased and followed, girls who could not find a way out of buildings. They are history and architecture. The one in our painted lady is an intimate part of her, long abandoned. I know its pulls, its wires and mechanisms, the ropes of its cage. I know primitive mechanized anatomy and can take it apart and put it back together, though I have some trouble understanding how to relate to kids my age. I'm just beginning to understand what I am and how I feel about Jane. She calls me a boy, but Mother says I'm a girl. Jane is the best babysitter I've ever had. She's better than the boys who live on Haight Street and whisper about the old elevator. I'm the elevator repairman. I'm fourteen years old the first time Jane tells me my mother is a criminal. I only stare. Standing eye-level to Jane's chest, I keep thanking my lucky stars. Jane doesn't like to wear clothes, since we have no air conditioning and aren't allowed to open windows, even in summer. Most of us hiding inside the painted lady would do anything to squeeze Jane's perfectly shaped areolas the size of salad plates. They're so big and pink, strikingly, earth goddess in their magnetism, drawing us toward her like planets in gravitational pull. Whenever she wants to control me and the boys and Mother's renters, who sleep in stacked bunkbeds honeycombed with strangers, she removes her blouse.

The Story of Jane

Collaged in shallow sculpts, real hair tacks into photographs of hair, lipstick applied to photographs of lips. In paintings of faces the size of women's faces, Jane wears vintage jewelry pierced through paper ears. Sketched faces, makeup applied to paper, powder, liquid eyeliner, mascaras scrawl on pages. Shellacked eyes hold gaudy eyelashes stroked by fingertips. Glued eyelashes curl from the pages as if from real eyes.

My eyelashes tickle the boy.

He shudders when he touches my pages.

The first time it happened, I didn't mean for my eyelashes to charm him. I was in the book with Jane. He was examining me along with other women, gazing into our mouths like vents, holes in holograms nestled inside the repurposed pizza box. The oily cardboard reeked of oregano. My mouth was scented with marinara sauce, whispering of fresh tomato, the velvet texture of olive oil.

My areolas smelled of old parmesan.

Blooming from busted fake-wood paneling, flowers with women's names were as tall as people. The boy never understood why the flowers were wonderful and yet worrying, never told his mother the photographed women inside the book looked like she did.

As he turned the pages through the screaming, through the shouting coming from the blood binding, he wanted to understand the story of Jane, the woman on the first pages, dragged out of her house and into the van with string to bind her hands before fingernails began scratching DNA evidence into her face.

He turned the brittle stained scratch-n-sniff pages smelling of decay with a sweet undertone that reminded him of chocolate. Other pages smelled of fear, blood, vomit, bleach, urine, and burning.

Where my dear Jane walked alone, her screams smelled of the night wind, exhaust from an old pipe, gasoline, and cigarettes. The boy leaned into my gaping mouth, scratched the page, and sniffed to inhale August sunlight on oaks and wild mint growing in ravines where I had wandered.

My face found its way into the *Book of Screams* several years ago. After Jane tried to save me, I was in the hospital for six weeks before I realized something had gone wrong. I couldn't believe what I was seeing. "Don't come near me!" I said to the boy, though he didn't hear.

Even now, I dream my body back, gridlocked in the death tunnel beneath the house on the hill. Here the vile odor of life cut short permeates elegant women like Jane, her hair styled in blood.

The dead, I understood their faces. I've scheduled multiple funerals this year, including my own.

When fear is a gift, Jane emerges from the dark house to fight for me.

Jane gets into the car with me and the crying girl, her handcuffed wrists straining.

Having fought for me, Jane no longer emerges from the dark house because the dark house emerges in the light where I see my best friend in the fireplace.

The victims' families face the photographic evidence with press releases about the way we disappear only to appear in the *Book of Screams* incriminating someone's husband, someone's father.

The book is bound with blood glue, pages of pressed and stretched dried skin, threaded with hair. The book smells putrid and sweet, but the boy doesn't want to talk about the smell because I've told him what it means. He loves the book too much. It's the kind of love that will make him a good cop or a successful murderer.

He sniffs the book secretly, not wanting his mother to know. He inhales deeply, huffing dried blood, old hair, perfume, and tissue. He sniffs bloody faces, fissures, inhaling the air inside the sockets of my gouged-out eyes.

Our families study the stars at night, knowing we are all love stories, but in some love stories, things happen that have nothing to do with love. Sometimes, through no fault of their own, love stories become the walls of condemned houses painted with clusters of flowers of women's names.

One of the flowers has my name, the purple iris, weeks before the demolition so that the city tears down painted flowers, not blood-stained walls.

Search the entire room for Natalie, and there are no signs she is there, behind the paint, under the floorboards with me. If you see us in Deep Flowers like shadows, part of the underground artists' big picture machine, the petals make you mine: the pink, yellow, orange, purple, violet, magenta, red, blue, green, toxic neon, and white.

The woman in black lace cartwheeling over my unmarked grave, another aspiring singer, haunts the magnificent Art Deco Theater condemned in Los Angeles. Men who make films about us call themselves underground artists for stealing unclaimed corpses of murdered women to make snuff films in reverse.

Out of their underground movies, a new Hollywood — born of desiccated, desecrated remains — reanimates the dead through makeup, CGI, and lighting.

Broken bodies untangle, hydrated, breathing.

The captured walk free with unmurdered women rewound to life.

I walk backward on rewind with women and girls I love.

Jane is with us, so is Natalie.

Second chances play in reverse. Our end is beginning.

My long brittle corpse recomposes into a daughter dancing.

Painted Ladies

Architecture holds mysteries. Old elevators are often forgotten like dreams. Perhaps only squatters and architects understand houses have lives and can be kidnapped and abused by tyrants. Buildings have memories and personalities. Painted ladies, the grand dames of San Francisco, have had so many lovers that this house on Haight Street has been bought and sold, stolen and repossessed, more than anyone knows.

I want to go back to find Jane. That's why I keep telling this story.

I keep going back to San Francisco to stand in front of the house, just remembering and wondering what happened to Jane. The people who lived in the neighborhood in 1978 aren't there anymore. The people who live there now are rich techies. They don't know me. They've never heard of Jane.

I long to go back to 1978, where inside the painted lady, Jane balances on a mountain of crocheted psychedelic pill-shaped pillows on her bed-shaped throne while playing Simon in the nude. Following the pattern of lights and sounds, she wins by losing herself in the game of electric lights, dancing blue, yellow, red, and green rapidly over her large pale pear-shaped breasts. Simon's tones, always harmonic, no matter the sequence, consist of an A major triad in second inversion, resembling a trumpet fanfare:

> E-note (blue, lower right);
> C#-note (yellow, lower left);
> A-note (red, upper right);
> E-note (green, upper left, an octave lower than blue, the sound of my child voice when I start to whimper, wanting Jane's attention).

Jane catches me gazing out the windows and says, "Don't do that."

Like all the rooms in Mother's house, Jane's room narrows to odd angles. The windows don't look out onto the outside world but onto other rooms and brick walls. It's as if someone has built a little house inside a big house. How could a house look so grand and large on the outside but feel so small and cramped on the inside? How could the windows on the outside not be here on the inside? I'm always wondering, trying to gaze through the windows at slivers where angled walls taper. Glimpsing through darkness, I wonder if bats are sleeping inside a cavern within the old house, between walls.

Games

I do everything Jane tells me to do, including repairing the elevator in the locked closet of her room. At first, it's just a game. No one even knows the elevator is there, until I find it by jimmying the lock. Mother tells us to leave the elevator alone, that it's broken and dangerous, that it will never run again. I obey Jane's every command. When she orders me to repair the elevator, this keeps me entertained. My mother is too busy evicting bad renters to pay attention. Now that Father has gone away, leaving Mother for another woman, Mother is so busy, trying to keep us clothed and fed. I get bored easily, unless I'm with Jane.

She's eighteen, a queen, roller skating topless in the house's twisty little rooms. I'm only useful and interesting to her when I get the elevator running.

I hold my breath and turn off all the lights to sit in darkness, until I force myself to remember Jane likes *The Muppet Show, Rockford Files,* and *Three's Company.* A crooked picture of Jimmy Carter hangs over the mantel in the den. My favorite game is Hungry, Hungry Hippos, but the game breaks soon after I take it from the box. I start to play other games, dangerous games, not like Hippos, but games like Slave and Elevator, games we make up in the house on Haight Street in the year of Atari when a dozen eggs costs 79 cents. Everyone has just started to play Space Invaders. Women are wearing smocked dresses with wedge boots or ballerina flats, and children don puppet mittens on chilly mornings. Jane has cocaine on her braces. Even though she's just a girl, she's the only person I know who inspires boys to stop playing Space Invaders. Jane keeps secrets. One day, she says, she will be the reason Jimmy Buffett stops drinking margaritas. I believe her.

Boys

I don't know why she's in charge of other boys, some of them older than she.

Now that Father is gone, Mother has enough problems without worrying about Jane and Jane's boys.

In Mother's house, Jane pays rent by caring for me. Jane's bedroom walls are painted the color of Pepto-Bismol. Her blankets and curtains are the green of oak leaves in summer. Jane adores pickles and sunflower seeds and boys with long hair. In spite of her mammoth breasts, she's slender with long legs and delicate toenails painted the color of the sky.

She invites boys in through the elevator, one by one, and presents them to me as if they are exotic pets or works of art. Kiss him, she says, and I do. One after another after another after another. The boys must do as she says in her room, where they can't make a sound.

When the first boy arrives by elevator, she tells him to stand beside the closet. And he does. When he talks, she tells him to shut up, and he does. This silent boy stares at her, waiting.

"Shut up," she says. "Shut up."

He's a sweet boy with a round face soft like dough. His light blue eyes sparkle, and we laugh because he obeys Jane's every command so well like Simon Says but Jane Says. On his third visit, he goes off script and starts talking about The Man. "The Man," the boy says, "is angry and waiting in the garage."

"Where?" asks Jane.

"At the bottom of the elevator."

Jane looks at me, as if I've betrayed our secret. While it's true that I'm the one who found the elevator and learned how to use it, I never told anyone but Jane, Mother, and Jane's boys. The old elevator was behind a locked door in Jane's room, a door we were told to "leave alone." It leads to the garage, full of junk and locked from the outside. Boys enter through a broken window but never men.

Who Are You?

"What's back there?" we ask Mother.

"Nothing," Mother says. "Leave it alone, okay?"

I pry open the old doors and bait the switch, the latch, the chain, and the buttons. The elevator groans down, down, down to the dank little garage crammed with junk, behind the building, where Mother and her tenants enter the painted lady by ladder and fire escape.

Jane and I wait in her room with the first boy, laughing, as the elevator chimes. The elevator ascends, creaking, rising slowly toward us. The doors shudder open onto a man older than Mother. Wearing a tailored suit, he impresses me with his shiny black shoes and well-groomed reddish mustache, a shade darker than his short, white hair, combed into ducktails shadowing generous sideburns.

"Who are you?" asks Jane.

"I'm the landlord. I own this property."

"What?" I ask. "This is my mother's house."

"No. You all aren't supposed to be here."

"What?" I ask.

The landlord winks as he says to the boy, "Get back inside that elevator."

The boy gazes softly into my eyes as the elevator doors close on him.

"What do you call this place?" the landlord asks, stroking his upper lip.

"Home," I say.

Why We Never Use the Front Door

Certain things start to make sense — why we never use the front door, why we have no mailbox, why Mother says for us not to be seen going in and out of the house. I always believed her, when she said it was ours. Now, I know better.

"It's not my fault," Jane says.

It's already too late. The landlord is inspecting all the little halls and rooms. "A warren," he says. "I never even knew this part of the house existed. Your mother is quite the clever architect." He smiles at Jane. "Of course, I won't be pressing charges, since Jane has enjoyed your little game."

I wonder how long Jane has known that Mother and I aren't supposed to be here. Was she just playing more games?

Mother is asleep now in her bed on the storage room's hardwood floor.

When Mother wakes in her makeshift bed of nesting blankets, she seems terrified to see the landlord. "All right, all right," she says. "The police won't be necessary. Just give us a chance to get our things?"

"Five minutes," the landlord says.

"Honey," Mother turns to me, "hurry. Get all your school clothes and little things — as many as you can carry, all in bags. Hurry!"

The landlord places his hand on his hip, inside his coat, and I notice a gun holstered. Jane is smiling. Her silly grin is the last I'll ever see of her face.

Haight Street Girls

I have no idea what happened to Jane. If anyone asks my opinion, I say Jane never left the house that night. She's still there, somewhere inside a part of the house no one has access to anymore. In my mind, she's forever in charge of me and so many others because she's a part of my dreams, even now, where I'm a man, just like she told me I would be.

Seems strange. Sure.

One minute it's 1978, and I'm repairing and then dismantling the old elevator in Jane's room in the house on Haight Street. One minute it's 1978, and suddenly everything is changing. In the year of Atari, the last year we will live in the house on Haight Street, we are being evicted by a man with a gun. Days later, after we have been forced out, Mother and I discover the landlord isn't the real owner of the painted lady. We confront the real owners at the front door. The elderly couple, rather well-to-do, assure us they have no idea who the landlord is and have never heard of him or Jane.

I remember Jane that night Mother and I were forced out, so cruelly, a dual event like the tarot teaches, a death card bringing life as the painted lady is about to give birth to us. Mother and I went out of the painted lady into the world, far away, her children becoming strangers to each other as we grow stranger in time. Time changes us into people we hardly recognize, evicting us from our old lives.

Jane appears in missing posters that fade away and disintegrate in rain.

Seems strange.

One girl. A teenage girl controlling so many people, even for a short time. One girl who has braces and refuses to wear a bra but skates nude through a house where she doesn't belong. Over time, I've come to understand her power.

The more vulnerable she makes herself, the less control anyone has over her.

The Prettiest Lost Girl in the City

The boy carries the *Book of Screams* through the house in the hills, that maze of stained carpets and scarred walls, into the house of dirty dishes, where his mother has no idea what he has done or what he is doing. He imagines himself as a detective working the case for the women and girls he finds in the *Book of Screams*. Scratching the pages, the boy releases scents and inhales them, placing his nose just above images of women whose eyes smell of tears in crumbling photographs, paintings, sketches, even holograms.

In that haze of hair draining to black water of the basement cellar, where I lost my dignity. Filmed without my consent, with other women, I have come to rage because no one knows it's happening.

My self-respect follows boots down a well where I slept ragged with the prettiest lost girl in the city. I still see her deep brown eyes. Men turned her degradation into gold until the movie industry became an indictment against them. Dressed in blood, tenderly, the girl picked up her knife and removed her clothes and her eyes.

Please help me understand why the house in the hills has the ambiance of a hemorrhage during a heart attack, the grace of gnats drowning in shallow wine. In puddles outside the shaded garage, water bugs skitter with cops securing rooms furnished with sadness before searching for smuggled opium.

The Hairstylist of the Damned makes Caligula seem gentle as he uses blood to sculpt my hair at night while hostage negotiators carry on, script by script, bargaining for the victims as if we are still alive.

Everyone talks about the house in the hills with its painted flowers and its bloody legends, but no one talks about Jane.

Jane emerges from the house and approaches the truck with the laughing man. I love Jane because I remember how she said she would fight for me after seeing my blood in the bathroom sink with those photographs at the bottom of the sink.

Men would rather go crazy than see the world as women who know why Jane no longer emerges from the house in the hills.

A shallow whine emerges from me when I open the wrong door and see my sister in the inglenook.

This was long ago. The moment is preserved in the *Book of Screams.*

The boy's mother calls to him as he pulls back the tab, lifting the flap on the page, where my sister waits in photographs, preserved under wax. The boy pulls one tab, and the inglenook opens to reveal her.

In the close-up of her face, her mouth is a door. The boy lifts a flap over her mouth, and her mouth opens so that he can stare inside it. Using a magnifying glass, he observes my anguish in close detail by expanding my sister's open mouth.

Can he see how much I wanted to save her? Can he guess how she waited for me and listened for me, knowing we were somewhere held inside the same house, separate but together, part of the same story?

On film, it keeps happening. As long as the film is out there, being shown, we can't make it stop.

In the *Book of Screams,* we are frozen in glue, shellacked in cement, sealers, and furniture polish, anything to hold us down. Images held in resin, we are varnished, lacquered women of similar fates. Sealed under glossy layers of polyurethane and epoxy, we flake and crack. The boy gently places us beneath his pillow.

I never escape what happened to my sister, and the boy will never stop dreaming of her alive. He thinks too much about her, as do other men. She was the prettiest lost girl in the city. I could never hold a candle to her beauty when strangers burned her clothes in the fireplace.

I will always be inside my sister's mouth when she screams.

This is not the story of the *Book of Screams*. This is a gift to you, a plea, a warning: you may not make it home tonight. An attacker is difficult to deal with in the Walmart parking lot while unlocking your car in the dark or pushing the cart. In the restroom with your pants around your ankles, the rapist is hard to escape. It's easy to forget your place when a man claiming to be a police detective asks you to follow him to where it's easy to forget fighting isn't always self-protection. The way he looks at you in the *Book of Screams,* how easy it is for men like him to get away with it.

The victims' families collect press releases about mothers burying their daughters, but the boy falls asleep with the *Book of Screams* gifting him surreal nightmares under his blanket, my death shroud where Martha Graham teaches dead girls to dance with the ghosts of their sisters until the boy wakes to find my face swollen beyond recognition.

Remember the dead, how their families chalked and drew and colored and spraypainted flowers all over the walls of the house in the hills? Instead of placing more flowers on victims' empty graves, they spraypainted giant flowers with the names of lost women and girls. Today, these painted flowers bloom as the house is hit by the wrecking ball, and the lost women head for the river, singing.

Even the headless are heady with their heads swinging in their hands clutching tangled hair styled in blood. They are singing sounds unheard as painted chalk flowers bloom, pollinating the city air with powder of painted petals. People all over the city breathe in the dust of destroyed flowers, the dust of the demolished house floating through ozone with human ashes, over the river cloud fog, pollinating the lungs of strangers.

Jack the Ripper schools the Zodiac Killer.

Ted Bundy shadows the Axeman.

Where Albert Fish sets a lovely dinner table for cannibals of the future, I have gone on a hunger strike.

The man who devoured pieces of me wanted to keep me after I died. Because there is a romance to cannibalism in the madness of the flesh, devouring me was devotion, a final indignity.

Never was I his, even when he ate me and my sister.

I was not me, and she was not her.

Rendered helpless, we all become something we are not: a body, a victim, a survivor.

If we survive and are brave enough to report the crime, we may be judged as bad victims for wearing the wrong type of panties.

Panties are political if you're sexy, and pretty, but if you are plain, your panties won't matter.

Since I was never the prettiest lost girl in the city, I disappeared from my life just as quietly as my name disappeared from the news, but my little sister was front-page because of her face.

To prepare for our final scene in the large bathroom called "the green room," marks on our faces were hidden by the makeup kit: cream foundation, powder, judicious lipstick. Long tresses hid bruises on our bodies, silken hair cascading over bruises like frilly black lace.

As the elder sister of the prettiest lost girl in the city, I was worth less than she was to those who paid for our destruction. She was the star of the movie, and I was background, disappearing like a prop.

When the insects in our mouths writhed, it was too late. Police removed flooring from the bathroom to find evidence, but they missed evidence in the car under the backseats and in the cracks in the house's walls, where our captor watched us.

What can I say of the man who murdered us?

Dr. Death was an angel compared to him.

Our murderer works on his victims as if he consults a cookbook authored by the Butcher of Rostov, a book on taxidermy by Ed Gein, and a book on arts and crafts by Jeffrey Dahmer, all while living in the house he remodeled using the architectural designs of H.H. Holmes.

Like the rest of his kind, he only celebrates acts that show him in the right light. There are acts he won't admit, acts he attempts to erase, for the same reason Bundy never admitted he was a necrophile.

How do I describe my sister now that she has been dismembered?

She's like the infamous unknown actress named Elizabeth Short, who became the Black Dahlia after fame cut her in half and exposed her body to strangers. People who saw her on death's stage kept mistaking her corpse for a mannequin in a field. Dehumanized, she was never forgotten in the way she would have been if society had found a way to humanize her.

November 17th was my time to die.

Because my sister had eyes like mine, I was estranged from her.

Strangled to release, again and again, I watched my captor gaze into the eyes of the prettiest lost girl in the city.

In the *Book of Screams,* pieces of me were preserved, collaged in taxidermy, shellacked, super glued, sealed in wax with remnants of my sister, who pretended not to know me to keep me alive.

Now, my little sister and I are ghosting Hollywood with the other women in the *Book of Screams.*

#Timesup breathed new life into us, helping us more than we could have ever imagined.

Haunting Hollywood, #MeToo came along and canceled auteurship in Los Angeles, until a group of underground artists reinvented auteurship by recruiting murdered girls like my sister and murdered women like me to re-enact our demise in reverse, no killer required.

Unmurdered, we spoke reverse sentences: *Eerf won ma I. Reverof evil lliw I. !Smaercs fo kooB eht depacse I,* until questions, the makers of legends, opened the gate to the reborn in the eyes of the curious boy devouring the *Book of Screams.*

Turning the pages, the boy questions how long drunken

strangers were galloping beneath the tree on the ground floor while gazing down into the basement windows to catch a glimpse of me, the third victim. (Pages 11 – 21 in the *Book of Screams.*)

"None of my business," drunken strangers would say in passing after gazing down at my tied ankles.

Hogtied. Elegantly dressed men with southern drawls said "hogtied" like it was nothing to the ghosts of moviegoers who assumed women dressed like me deserved to be tied with girls dressed like my sister.

In the movies, who can say what is real?

Wherever the shadow of Harvey Weinstein's deformed penis falls over the faces of a generation's most iconic women, there are miserable ways to become a survivor. Ladies fight back by smiling through pain, looking pretty while angry, and faking an orgasm.

In the *Book of Screams,* I am smiling at the boy to get him to see me as more than a tortured body.

He will see my eyes through generations yet unborn, but he will never see me as having hopes and dreams equal to his.

The *Book of Screams* is such a shitty book, the only way I can get close to the boy, who one day will be the father of my grandchildren, who will never know me.

As the boy becomes a man, I've wanted him to love me, not this way.

FINGER PAGES QUICKLY AND BE DO

-EVIDENCE-

FILE NO. Exhibit 23

NAME The Rape Machine

SECTIONS Weaponized Women; Hairs in an Envelope; Messages from My Body

Weaponized Women

When Sexualized Desecration is not just the name of a punk band from California that turns women into puppets on a string, after the horrors of Hamas, the Russian Rape Machine forces the question:

When does rape become genocide with its intent to destroy?

With objects.

With fingers, hands, any part of the body.

When an army can invade a person's body like it invades a foreign territory.

When invasion is never gender neutral.

When women are the battlefield.

When women are the most dreaded weapon.

When weaponized women are turned into objects of terrorism used against other women.

When Sexual Violence in Armed Conflict is rape, sexual slavery, forced prostitution, forced pregnancy, forced sterilization, forced abortion, sexual mutilation, and sexual torture.

When women who are raped deserve the support of other women, but they don't get the support of other women because they make other women uncomfortable.

When women who are raped are used as weapons by men against other women and are offensive to other women.

When women are used as messages.

When we get into trouble because we can't find a way to separate the message from the woman, the way she lived from the way she died, what happened to her body from who she was.

When every dead girl's body is a message written in broken legs, broken pelvises, bloody underwear.

When what happens to one girl's body is a message to all girls.

When not every woman wants to hear this message, or is willing to read the broken legs, broken pelvises, and bloody underwear for what they are saying to her. So, she decides to show herself as another kind of woman by rejecting the raped and nodding to the rapist as if to say, *This never happened, but if it did, it happened for a reason to certain women and certain girls. I'm on your side. I'm not like her, and she's not me. I know you're a good man. You would never do to me and to good girls what you did to the bad women and bad girls like them.*

When we can't reject the message without rejecting those sacrificed to send us the message.

When we're all puppets on a string because your broken legs are my broken legs — your blood, my blood.

When women found with legs and hands tied to their beds, vaginas stabbed with knives and internal organs removed tell us something we hear after their voices are silenced.

Hairs in an Envelope

It's easier to talk to you, a stranger, about why you don't scream and why you have to prove it with hairs in an envelope, with stains, with laundry and fingernail clippings to tell the story more than words.

Messages from My Body

You might know me as Gisèle Pelicot, the raped wife. I'm more famous in France than my infamous husband. People know my name and have forgotten his.

Like other women who have suffered in secret, I had to learn to listen to my body. My body was trying to communicate something I needed to hear. For years, I didn't understand how it wanted to heal me and save me.

Mysterious bruises were messages from my body, which was trying to tell me the truth about my husband and what my attackers were doing, night after night when I was drugged, sleeping.

My husband was lying to me. My body was my only friend, and yet he invited other men to invade my body without my knowledge as he turned our house into a rape machine.

After drugging my wine, so I wouldn't remember, my husband, who thought of everything, filmed these attacks, inviting strangers to take part in an online forum called "Without Her Knowledge."

Rituals strangers had to follow, my husband's rules, instructed them to wash their hands in hot water until their skin was warm to the touch so as not to wake me with their cold fingers.

In videos, stripped naked and filmed countless times without my consent or knowledge, I'm a nameless woman, violated in immeasurable ways while sleeping. All for his pleasure and the pleasure of strangers he welcomed into our home.

When I was Sleeping Beauty, I was my rapist's wife, the mother of his children, the woman he called a saint, the woman he called a slut. I'll never understand why my rapist husband didn't rape me with his body but with the bodies of other men. Maybe there are some things not worth understanding.

My body tried telling me in bruises, tenderness, and strange pains inside enigmatic bleeding. I once caught a disease that people are ashamed of catching. This was another message I couldn't understand.

After the authorities watched the films and discovered my name, they showed the films to me. They pitied me and invited me to keep my identity a secret by hiding my face from the world the way news organizations blurred the faces of murdered women in crime scenes and war zones in images of the dead.

I said, "No. I refuse to hide in shame."

"Why?" they asked.

How could I make such a choice?

Ask yourself: Who are you protecting, and why?

Why should I feel ashamed of what was done to me when I'm innocent of the crimes committed against me? I'm as innocent as my body, which can't be blamed for what was done to it. This violation has already happened hundreds of times.

I survived.

I'm still me, no matter what was done to my body.

I'm not hiding my face. Neither should you. No matter what was done to us, we're still here. We're alive.

Acknowledgements

This project was made possible by a H.A.D (Humanities, Arts, and Design) Grant from Oklahoma State University and by a Hargis Fellowship at the OSU Doel Reed Center for the Arts in Taos, New Mexico.

Many thanks to Patrick Davis, Peter Campion, Cory Firestine, and to Unbound Edition Press for their support.

Some of these pieces appeared (in various forms) in the following journals:

Another Chicago Magazine

Big Other

Coffin Bell

The Experiment Will Not Be Bound Anthology

Fiction International

Flash Frog

Fugue

Get Bent: Bending Genre Anthology

Hullabaloo Mag

JMWW

Landlocked

Lake Effect

Little Fiction

Moon City Review

New Ohio Review

The Pinch

Phare Magazine

Revel

Sage Cigarettes

Shotgun Honey

Tupelo Quarterly

About the Author

Aimee Parkison is a writer of experimental prose known for her revisionist narratives about women. She is widely published and the recipient of numerous awards and fellowships, including the FC2 Catherine Doctorow Innovative Fiction Prize, the Kurt Vonnegut Prize from *North American Review*, the Starcherone Prize for Innovative Fiction, a Christopher Isherwood Fellowship, a North Carolina Arts Council Fellowship, a Writers at Work Fellowship, a Puffin Foundation Fellowship, and a William Randolph Hearst Creative Artists Fellowship. She currently teaches creative writing in the MFA/PhD program at Oklahoma State University, where she has been awarded a Regents Distinguished Research Award and has been named a DaVinci Creativity in Education Fellow. To learn more about her work, visit www.aimeeparkison.com.

About the Type and Paper

Designed by Malou Verlomme of the Monotype Studio, Macklin is an elegant, high-contrast typeface. It has been designed purposely for more emotional appeal.

The concept for Macklin began with research on historical material from Britain and Europe dating to the beginning of the 19th century, specifically the work of Vincent Figgins. Verlomme pays respect to Figgins's work with Macklin, but pushes the family to a more contemporary place.

This book is printed on natural Rolland Enviro Book stock. The paper is 100 percent post-consumer sustainable fiber content and is FSC-certified.

Body of Evidence was designed by Eleanor Safe and Joseph Floresca.

Unbound Edition Press champions honest, original voices. Committed to the power of writers who explore and illuminate the contemporary human condition, we publish collections of poetry, short fiction, and essays. Our publisher and editorial team aim to identify, develop, and defend authors who create thoughtfully challenging work which may not find a home with mainstream publishers. We are guided by a mission to respect and elevate emerging, under-appreciated, and marginalized authors, with a strong commitment to advancing LGBTQ+ and BIPOC voices. We are honored to make meaningful contributions to the literary arts by publishing their work.

unboundedition.com